MARGO OF THE BELLS

Also by Melanie Greene

Dunway Siblings Series

Feather in Her Cap *(Jeannie & Brendan)*

Twelve Scorching Days *(Sarita & Scorch)*

Margo of the Bells *(Margo & Karl)*

Pier 3 Coffee Series

Mocha for Mateo *(Alicia & Mateo)*

Cappuccino for Callie *(Abraham & Callie)*

Latte for Leyla *(Austin & Leyla)*

Curiosity *(Amity & Josh) - Callie-related story*

Roll of the Dice Series

Rocket Man *(Serena & Dillon)*

Ready to Roll *(Janice & Miguel)*

Eye of the Tiger *(Natalie & Evan)*

Let the Good Times Roll *(Chloe & Gabriel)*

Roll of a Lifetime *(Rachel & Theo)*

Roll Play *(Kim-ly & Tómas)*

On a Roll *(Gillian & Vic)*

Roll in the Hay *(Anton & Cisco) - available to subscribers or as a bonus in the Roll of the Dice novella anthology*

MARGO OF THE BELLS

MELANIE GREENE

First print edition: October 2022

Margo of the Bells/by Melanie Greene

Cover Design by Melanie Greene

ISBN: 978-1-941967-44-7

To Pops
Happy 80th Birthday!

CHAPTER

ONE

MARGO

Wind, sea spray, sky. Dip oar, stroke, fly.

As my brother and I propel our tandem kayak from one swell to the next across the winter-cool sea, I relish moving away from everything that awaits us on shore. Even if it's for only one more stroke, it's a freedom I need to store up before the holidays get fully underway.

We'd left Austin early, but still managed to get caught in traffic snarls all along our route. As soon as we'd pulled into our coastal hometown of Rockport, I'd persuaded Cole we should zip down to the bay for a paddle. On the water, I stretched my wingspan as wide as the horizon. My heart thumped, reliable as the tides.

I needed the hour on the water before we washed up into a mess of Thanksgiving tasks and family obligations. Before I faced all the questions: what would I do next; why not just move back home; how could I say no to staying, when I didn't have any other plans?

As if I hadn't explained to everyone how I craved journeys, not destinations.

As if even if I wanted a destination, Rockport would be on my list.

It wasn't until we'd run aground on the beach and were stowing our oars that Cole said, "Check your email when we're home. I signed you up for something."

"You did what?"

He passed over a water bottle. "Don't get defensive."

"When have I ever been defensive?"

He snorted. "You want the list just from this week, or is this more of a lifetime overview kind of thing?"

I hefted the stern of the boat. He took the bow, and started reciting a needlessly long list of my occasional snippy moments. "That time I asked where the can opener was. Your whole deal with the university bursar, who, let me reiterate, did not have it in for you. Your diatribe when that bank teller misgendered me."

"The bursar did so have it in for me. Ask Nina about the supposed form letter I got first semester senior year, compared to hers."

Cole snorted again, checked we'd lashed the kayak to the roof properly, and tossed me the car keys.

I ignored his criticism. We didn't normally bicker, but odd little cracks between us had been appearing more often in the run-up to Thanksgiving. Or more pertinently, in the run-up to the first time in my twenty-four years that we wouldn't be living together.

Cole was a few years older than me; growing up we hadn't been especially close. He tended to hang with our older sisters, and as for me? I sometimes paired tight with our youngest sister, but until I'd learned better, I was mostly hanging out at church. And when I was seventeen and that turned into a disaster, I boomeranged right into Cole's orbit, and hadn't left since.

We'd done a lot of turning into adults together. He'd taken a gap year and lived at home during the first stages of his medical transition, which meant he was around during my crisis, the most supportive sibling imaginable exactly when I needed him. We both moved to Austin after I finished high school, and ended up graduating from UT a semester apart. Lived together throughout college and then a pandemic.

And now I was isolating myself in Rockport from Thanksgiving until January, helping out our Uncle Bill with tourist season and building savings to fund my next moves. Meanwhile Cole would be back in Austin, hopefully job hunting his way out of the customer service job he despised.

Safe to say we were fretting about each other. I wanted the world to not be a judgmental jerk and to never question his identity. He wanted me to embrace my interests without being scared I'd lose everything if I lost a defining passion.

"You take care of you and I'll take care of me," he'd said more than once in the lead-up to the holiday season. And damn if it didn't cut deeper through my protective knots every time. I was the proudest little sister ever, seeing Cole so confident about his future. And also, I was nothing but a sack of nerves about not having him in my life every day. That boomerang thing I'd done back in high school brought us close, but also left me too ready to hitchhike along his path instead of forging my own.

I needed to figure my damn self out. To embrace a passion of my own choosing.

Which I would. Soon. It was on my list of things to do.

Apparently Cole was impatient for me to check it off. I

paused before the final turn onto our parents' street. "Okay, what's this email?"

"Promise me first you'll do it."

"Cole."

"Gogo." His voice held a bite of laughter as he teased out my family nickname, the one they used to say I didn't slow down enough to decide if I was running away from something or to something else.

I tightened my grip on the steering wheel, which sent him collapsing in mirth against the passenger window.

I narrowed my eyes at him.

"Margo, listen," he said, all pointed and deep in imitation of our dad's lecture voice. "I'm only looking out for you."

"And I'm only telling you that you're not the only grown-ass Dunway in this car, so I'll look out for myself, thanks very much."

He bent to gather all the detritus of our road trip as I parked in front of our family home. "Fine. But keep in mind you're the one who said that discovery is sometimes rediscovery."

My shoulders were bunching up tighter with every too-patient word. "I was talking about *Drag Race Down Under*."

He waved that off. "Nevertheless. When I saw the call for help, I knew it was perfect way for you to rediscover your passion, like you keep claiming you're going to do."

"What perfect way? Help who? Why do I have to help anyone when I'm the one looking for a passion?"

Cole blinked faux-innocent eyes at me. "This belligerence of yours is why I made you promise before you found out. Also, I told Mama already, so you can't get out of it. You're going to spend the next month as part of the hand-bell choir at St. Luke's Episcopal."

He sauntered inside like he hadn't just slung an off-key albatross around my neck.

For the record, back when I was a teen, I wasn't the only Dunway to leave St. Patrick's Catholic Church.

What I had been, was the one most likely to haunt the place up until my public disillusionment, what with my youth groups, and my work in the after-school daycare, and the voice and handbell choir rehearsals, and, of course, Mass. Even my volleyball team practiced at St. Pat's.

But then I left, and so did the rest of the family. Difference was, most of them pretty quickly found St. Luke's and embraced the Episcopalian congregation. I appreciated their solidarity in leaving St. Pat's, in an abstract way, when I wasn't busy reeling from all my severed connections. But I never followed their lead, no matter how much tolerance and progressivism they claimed for the new place.

Cole attended, which confused me some. Not often, but he'd tag along for the occasional service during our visits home. He'd shrug or wrinkle his nose or otherwise send the message that he was fine keeping the peace. Until now, he hadn't pressed me to do the same.

Last Easter, I'd outright asked. "I don't get how you aren't bothered on, like, a personal level, by the bigotry that's been spread in the name of organized religion. How are you cool visiting that place?"

He literally rolled his eyes at me. "Gogo, you're acting like I have two damns to spare for what people I don't know or care about think and say about me. I had to learn years ago not to heed any of that. You matter, our family matters, my community matters. Whether or not some guy in the next pew affords me my whole identity? Not my problem. Dad and Mama love St. Luke's. They care about their faith —not as much as they care about me, which they always made clear. But for me? I cut religion loose as soon as I realized how bad it could serve me."

"So when you were, like, eleven?" It was around age eleven when Cole told me he was a boy. When he was in high school, he came out to the rest of the family, but I'd always thought it savvy of him to tell me and our youngest sister before too many of our preconceived notions about gender solidified. Emmeline and I were ready to follow his lead on his name and pronouns as soon as he asked.

"Please, I was eight. I just had a few years of pondering to do before I said much. My view is, it doesn't matter which church I'm at. I listen to services like they're a kind of boring story slam someone dragged me to."

"Cole, Jesus."

"Yep. Jesus. He may be the ultimate judge of the story slam, but since I don't care who advances in the competition, I'm not seeking out his opinion either. That's a difference between us, you know, Gogo."

"What is?"

"I can walk in to any congregation or denomination and not let it affect me, because I chose to let all that go."

I bristled like how very dare he with this big brother wisdom. Telling me I hadn't let go of my faith. "So did I."

"No." He bumped my shoulder. "That's a story you've been rehearsing for years now. But you didn't have a choice. You had to leave, as the only right and sustainable decision, but you weren't just breezing out of St. Patrick's, Margo. It was a true loss. You ripped away from something that had been important to you, maybe even precious. I think there's a reckoning there, and I think you'll be glad if you stop glaring at me and just go ahead and face it."

And, I guess, since I'd made a point of ignoring his opinions, now he was using the time I was stuck in Rockport to force the issue. The interfering brat.

I did my best to stay in the wind until Thanksgiving, settling into a staff room at my uncle's hotel and re-familiarizing myself with the place. Like most of us Dunways, I'd worked for Uncle Bill off and on during high school, but I'd ended up doing it more than Cole or our sisters in the long, long months between fleeing St. Pat's and heading to Austin for college. It had been a refuge when I needed it, which made it hard to refuse when Uncle Bill asked me to help out during the holiday season.

Winters were big business on the Gulf Coast, especially with all the birders following the flocks to Aransas National Wildlife Refuge, just on our doorstep. Soon my days would resound with advice to visitors about Whooping Cranes, terns, plovers and spoonbills. Uncle Bill's hotel was at capacity, and he needed someone with experience—me— to help manage all that meant.

But once I showed up on Thanksgiving morning, it was open season as far as my family was concerned.

"Bill says he'll make it your year-round job, you know," Mama told me.

I was wrist-deep in cornbread stuffing mix when she ambushed me, meaning I had not a chance in hell of fleeing. "I know, but like I told him, I'm only here for the season."

She looked at me like I'd sworn to defrost the turkey then left it in the deep-freeze on purpose. "I just want you to think about it. There's nothing wrong with knowing your options, Margo Adele Dunway."

First Cole pushing me to commit to the handbell choir. And now our mom middle-naming me about a permanent job. I wasn't going to rethink all my plans just cause they thought they knew what was best or easiest for me. "Can you check the small oven? The pie smells done."

Aunt Maxima came in and smooched everybody's cheeks, pausing to cup my face in her hands and smooth back my hair. "If you don't like that room at Bill's hotel, you tell me. My garage apartment is empty, so you can move in any time. Now, it's not furnished, but that doesn't mean we can't come up with everything you need between the lot of us. I've already got a dining set sitting under blankets in my spare room."

"Thank you, Max, but I'm not here to stay."

Whether she heard me, I don't know, but suddenly the kitchen overflowed with chatter about which person had what castoff furniture I could use.

It was entirely too much; no one believed what I was saying with every ounce of my heart. I loved them, but a month of gently suffocating in the town where I'd lost my whole overly idealistic identity? That was about all I could handle.

"Okay, Parsley, come on, baby." I helped my golden retriever hop down from my truck. She didn't normally need assistance with the leap, but I didn't know how careful we needed to be about activity after her surgery. Dr. Meyers had passed over a pile of instructions when I picked her up, but I'd been distracted cataloging my poor pup's energy level and feeling heartsick at the size of the bandage on her leg. I knew I'd have to carefully read the ream of paperwork before I'd be comfortable with her bouncing in and out of vehicles or hurtling head-first into the waves again.

We needed to sit tight and quiet at home. Get past this scare before more big adventures.

And, yeah, I was projecting onto my dog, but I wouldn't forget anytime soon the sight of Parsley crumpled on the trail, like a clump of golden fur that had been dropped from a great height. Which wasn't far off from what had happened when she'd collided with an ATV as they both crested a sand dune. My knees had given out as the force pulled her leash from my hand, and I'd sunk to the beach.

She'd flown impossibly high before landing on the bed of sea oats. The ATV driver had helped me get her to the truck and held her still while we raced to Dr. Meyer's surgery, swearing up and down he'd never again break beach rules about off roading.

I'd believed him. His shock was genuine. But I had trouble summoning any words of reassurance while my dog's hip fracture was being evaluated. I'd texted later, assuring him she was fine, his contrition wasn't necessary, he could stop asking me for penance.

She *was* fine. What mattered was that she was fine. I guided her inside and settled her on our sofa, then dashed back out for the bag of wound care supplies and the groceries I'd snagged on the way to the vet, so I wouldn't have to leave her anytime soon.

The house had been damn lonely without her. No tap-tapping paws heading to investigate if the food bowl had magically re-filled itself. No deep doggy sighs as we settled in our respective beds at night. No one wagging her way up to express appreciation of my musical genius when I sang one of the many little ditties I made up about her.

I caught myself too many times singing, "Are you going to be my best pup? / Parsley Moore, my pup very fine," and not being answered by a wet nose nudging into my hand, as if to certify that yes, absolutely, no finer pup existed. I'd missed having her around to share in my delight at how phenomenal and good she was.

I'd waited so long—too long—after my divorce to adopt the dog my ex never wanted, but I always did. Too long living adrift before I settled into being single again. Or single for the first time, really, since Susanne and I got married the same weekend as our college graduation, and every facet of adulthood, until our divorce when we were twenty-seven, included her.

I spent over a year deliberately quashing my habit of deferring to her opinion—or what I thought would be her opinion—on anything I wanted in my life. It sucked, but the day I adopted Parsley was an anchor I could hang onto. A day I knew I'd finally let my own desires take precedence.

My relief at that moment of independent thought said too much, but I relished this new version of myself, too. I understood myself in a deeper and more accepting way. Everything I wanted now, I wanted with absolute certainty. I build my world to fit the life I wanted, and I'd be ready when it came along.

Parsley plopped her head in my lap, breaking me out of my morose mood. She'd investigated her tragically empty bowls before returning to lean into my touch, and hadn't seemed to struggle with any of the movement. I stroked her silky ears while scanning the discharge papers.

"Well, looks like you're cleared for short walks."

Her tail wagged at her favorite 'W' word and I answered her eagerness with our beach-strolling song as I grabbed her leash and met her at the door.

The walk from my place to St. Luke's was still a bit far for Parsley, so after wiping down her sandy paws, I left her with a dental chew and many apologetic belly rubs. Her soulful eyes worried at me as I set out, and part of me ached about that.

The rest of me, though? I only had this one rehearsal with my handbell choir before the first Sunday of Advent, and I was going into it two steps behind thanks to the time I'd spent at the emergency vet.

Most of my ringers had been with me for a while, and I knew they could roll with challenges. But a donor gifted St.

Luke's with an extra octave's worth of bells, which meant adding new players. I'd recruited and trained three before Parsley's injury, but the last one I was taking on faith that she hadn't completely forgotten her skills from years back.

I'd dug up music that would work if my upper octaves could manage four-in-hand ringing. Organized bell assignments according to each player's strengths. Spent part of my Thanksgiving creating a playlist of the tunes to help out the aural learners. The timeframe was tight, no question, but I was confident I could get the bells to resound from the chancel with hope and celebration.

Excitement. It was excitement beating against my ribs, not stress; I was eager to get this new, fuller, group up and running.

After setting up the bells and music stands on the padded tables, I greeted the old guard of my handbell players—we called them the Three Graces, though only two of them were named Grace. While everyone moved into place, they caught me up on their Thanksgivings, which was just another excuse to scold me for declining their various pity invites in favor of spending the holiday alone.

They thought it was pride, me refusing to admit I was lonely for the holiday. But I could admit that. It was my stubbornness that kept me from falling in with others' traditions when what I craved was a tradition of my own.

I paced the area between the bell tables and my podium, using my free space to direct the ringers' attention to the expanded setup. The new octave was made up of the five new bells above high G, and seven more in bass clef, which meant two additional players at either end of the spectrum. "Okay, thanks for being on time, everyone. And especially thanks to our new ringers—Paul, Kay, Margo, and Julieta—for being here, and on time. You'll get so used to it you'll roll your eyes at me like everyone else, but as a reminder: rehearsal starts on time, whether you're here or not. So be here, or you might miss these inspiring chats of mine."

Most people smiled or chuckled at that, but Margo's eyes were narrowed, her expression flat. I wouldn't have recognized her from back when she was in my handbell choir at St. Patrick's Catholic, and not just because she hadn't had the neon orange streak in her wavy dark hair back then. That whole time was—well, on top of being in the middle of my tumultuous marriage, I hadn't exactly settled seamlessly into that particular music director job. Just seeing Margo Dunway's name on the list of people answering the call for handbell players had slammed me back to those days of self-doubt and learning to speak up. I wanted to check in with her about it all, but she'd signed up, so she must be at ease with everything. And I knew she knew the instrument. And I'd run out of time to fill the choir. So I'd brought her in.

But it looked like she wasn't eager to stick around after rehearsal for that chat I'd emailed to suggest.

I went on with my rehearsal spiel. "There's a notation cheat sheet at the back of your music packets. The first two pieces we'll work on are mostly ring and damp, or table damp for you low bells, with some echo and some thumb dampening. If you need to grab a highlighter or pencils to mark your lines, there are a few in that tray behind A5 B5. Otherwise known as Grace, right?"

The quietest of the Graces smiled around at everyone, even the dour Margo beside her. "Also the sharp."

"Beg your pardon, yes. A5, A#5, B5. Which reminds me, I've been doing some transcription for pieces for Gaudete Sunday, now that we have three lovely octaves to ring. I'll engrave those this week. So if you're wondering when you'll get a chance to trill or echo, don't worry, that's on the way."

On the other side of Margo, Church Council Grace pumped her fist. Down at the bass clef table, though, Matt the Grace lifted worried eyebrows. I gave him a slight nod to show I understood his worries; I knew he didn't yet believe my assurances that he could handle the new, larger bells. Beside him, his son Paul rested a hand on his shoulder, and I squashed any impulse I had to envy their easy connection.

The new ringers, interspersed as they were with my usual choir, were young and brightly dressed compared to the two-octave choir's cohort. The vibe was that of a slightly ragtag group of strangers who'd been stranded together, which might sound daunting. But to me, pulling together disparate people so they not only harmonized, but enhanced each other, was the catnip of conducting.

I took my place on the podium in front of them, flattened open my notes for our rehearsal schedule, and invited all eyes onto me as I led them through warmups.

CHAPTER
THREE

MARGO

Walking into St. Luke's choir rehearsal room was like being shrouded by a dripping fog of nostalgia. Putting on the ringer's gloves, scooting behind the bell tables, setting myself up at F5 F#5 G5 G#5 as instructed by a woman named Grace.

And then? Fuck me, because who turned around to direct us but that two-faced, closed-minded, above-it-all man Mr. Moore. I swear I flushed from head to toe and back again. Talk about the nightmare of Christmas Past come to haunt me with the rattling chains of every reason I'd resisted this gig from the minute Cole thrust it at me.

Mr. Moore smiled all affable, acting like there was no disconnect between the Karl at St. Luke's Rockport who emailed with genial logistics, and the choir director who'd stood alongside the leadership of St. Pat's when they turned my private life into a public shaming.

Not to get all dramatic about it, but when I was a teen, St. Pat's was my sanctuary. Like a lot of people with many siblings, we tended to pick one thing and make it our defining identity. Larissa was the athlete; Jeannie was the quiet one; Sarita was the partier; Cole was the fandom nerd; Emmeline was the scholar. I was the devout one. And a big part of that, for me, was the music. I loved choir rehearsals and performances, my soul sang to sacred music, it all fed my faith. And now, on top of all the other sense-memories sucking me into my unfortunate past, I had to face that when I was in high school, I'd harbored an entirely unfortunate and, okay, inappropriate, crush on the new choir director.

I wasn't some clueless teenager sitting around making Indiana Jones eyes at him or anything. For one thing, I'd known he was married; conductors spend a lot of time waving their be-ringed hands around in front of you. Mostly I'd been indulging in fantasies about growing up. Larissa'd been about to get married, which maybe is why I spent too long envisioning who would be my own perfect guy. Sure as hell it wouldn't be one of the jerks I'd been in school with all my life, especially not after overhearing their juvenile jokes. Meanwhile, here was this supremely cute young man spending hours in front of me every week, being focused and engaging and grown up in a way I'd have loved to be.

At twenty-four, looking back at seventeen, it was easy to figure out I hadn't lusted after Mr. Moore himself, never mind how fucking cute he was, with his neat beard and deep eyes and flexing arm muscles. And that one pair of jeans he sometimes wore at rehearsals, standing just high enough on his dais to let my imagination take some unwarranted leaps.

No, what I'd really craved was access to the power to make adult decisions. To live out my future in my own terms.

And then? Who sauntered past my craving heart but

Garrett, the most aloof boy in youth group. It turned out he wasn't so aloof once it was just the two of us. When we took long walks along the beach after Mass, ducking between sand dunes to kiss, and then to touch. Or when our friends, whose jokes suddenly seemed exciting instead of juvenile, covered for us sneaking off to empty rooms.

Garrett also, it turned out, was not so aloof when it came to staying quiet about my abortion. Which I found out in front of my choir and my family and our entire congregation, when Father James's sermonizing about sin came a millimeter shy of naming me.

Damn Garrett anyway. He and the rest of our friends in the youth choir had turned to stare at me. As if to reinforce exactly who the priest was describing in all the worst Old Testament ways. And all the while, Mr. Moore stood there by his piano, hand half-raised to cue our next hymn.

I'd bolted. Choir robe flapping behind me, clear as a flag from a sinking boat, and I didn't wait for my family to catch up. I was a mile down the road before Dad pulled over beside me and emerged to give me a long hug.

Later, after Uncle Bill and Cole helped me sit down with Dad and Mama to tell them the whole story, Dad returned my choir robe to Mr. Moore. "And that's the last time any Dunway sets foot in St. Patrick's," he'd said. Even my godmother Aunt Max followed that decree.

They'd migrated to the Episcopalians, and told me all the good things about it. Uncle Bill met his partner Sam at a St. Luke's LGBTQ+ meetup. Larissa's old track coach spearheaded the Church Council's beach cleanup efforts. They served decent tea and coffee after services.

And good for them for all of that, but they also hired Mr. Moore to conduct the choir. My body wanted to bolt again, but I was hemmed in by the close quarters: bell tables in front of me, the wall behind me, and all the other ringers elbow to elbow beside me. Mr. Moore—no, Karl; I might be trapped but I could respond like an adult—kept on talking, all oblivious like he wasn't some sort of devil sucking me into his quicksand plans. My hands were sweating in my bell ringers gloves, and I didn't know how to leave.

Fuck that. I wouldn't run again. I didn't deserve to feel any shame. No one who sought an abortion deserved to be shamed, which is one of the things Cole had repeated as he and the clinic escort had guided me past the gauntlet of histrionic protestors at the Planned Parenthood we'd driven over three hours to reach. It had been a too-new idea to me at the time, that rejection of shame, but I'd internalized it since. And vocalized about it—reproductive rights were too vital to stay quiet about, especially not with the way my state and my nation had destroyed what little access we'd once had. If I were seventeen and pregnant today, taking Uncle Bill's loan and Cole's dead name ID to pass as nineteen would only be steps one and two of a long, difficult process to obtain the medical care I needed to terminate.

So, no. The world was noticeably worse than when I was a teenager, but that didn't mean I had to be petulant about it. I flexed my fingers to settle my gloves, and grabbed the F and G bells. I had the right to take up space with my presence, and with the pealing of the bells.

Karl bloody Moore ran us through warmups, settling us all into the rhythm of ring and damp, ring and damp, gesturing to us each in turn as if his limbs weren't the least weighed down by his complicity.

And damn it all, because before my mind caught up to the blanketing feeling of peace, my body was reacting like everything around was charming and familiar. Never mind the past, never mind the reappearance of the choir director who should be the one owning his shame, never mind the running list of complaints I was already preparing for Cole.

Apparently all that mattered to my ridiculous soul was the sound ringing through the room. One of the Graces beside me sent me an approving little nod, and the bell handles fit easy as ever in my hand, and the longer we played, the more I was tempted to forget every grievance and to just enjoy making music.

I'd shaken off that blanket of peace by the time I got home and cornered Cole in the kitchen. "Did you know?"

"Know what?" He handed me his dish of flan, which only mollified me somewhat.

"That it's the same choir director."

Cole straightened. "Wait, what? No way."

"Way."

My deadpan tone didn't wither Cole's smile one bit. I reached across the island and snagged his beer. I found myself gripping the bottle like I was tempted to lob it hard at a concrete wall. Like shattering it into tiny shards would have any rebounding effect on my delighted brother.

I finished the drink and narrowed my eyes. "Is that why you made me promise to do the handbells?"

"So you'd run into Cutie McChoirface again? You think I'm that diabolical?"

"You want me to run that question past the sibling chat?"

He waved that off. "A bunch of biased sisters, that's my curse in life."

"Look, Cole. You and your story slam philosophy may not get worked up about it, but for all y'alls feel-good tidbits about St. Luke's, it's always going to be a product of the people in charge."

"Sure. And?"

"And no place that puts Karl Moore in charge is a place I want to be."

Cole, quiet for a moment, cut us each more flan. He sighed. "I hear you, but answer me this. Why didn't you leave as soon as you saw McChoirface today?"

"You made me promise."

"Sure, but what was the real reason? Did you hate ringing again like you swore was inevitable?"

I got water for me and another beer for Cole, trusting my silence to answer him.

"Did Cutie McChoirface beg you to stay?"

I snorted. "I left before he could say a word to me."

"So, in summary, you had fun playing and no one was mean to you and you are beginning to finally accept that big brother knows best and this genius idea of mine might give you back something—I don't know whether that's faith or just a bunch of other nerds to ring bells with—you might be missing?"

I shoved my empty plate towards him, took my drink, and left.

On Sunday morning, I drove to St. Luke's earlier than the rest of the family, so I could get ready with the other ringers for service. I almost felt an annoying sense of community, just from entering the sanctuary with everyone. The space was filled with that omnipresent dusty church light, and the wood and wood polish smells, and all kinds of greenery as if we lived in some alpine place rather than smack in the middle of the Gulf Coast. The chorister robes and performance gloves and some ineffable Christmas vibe brought my younger, more faithful and trusting self too much to the fore. I kept trying to catalogue anything new or different. My fellow ringers.

The yellow-pale wood of the pews instead of the dark oak of St. Pat's. The sprig of holly pinned to Karl's robes, which was a flair no one could have gotten away with back then.

Speaking of something not new or different: Karl.

Never mind my reluctance, or my irritation, or my desire to not get mired in the past. I still had to pay attention to my conductor. The instrument wasn't new to me, but this music was. I couldn't avoid focusing on him.

And damn me to hell and back, because now I wasn't thinking about Karl's currently bare ring finger, or the Advent homily, or even Cole's smirking told-you-so face. Because he did tell me so. I threw my 'I want to follow my own passions' wish out into the universe and what it tossed back was an intense memory of a time when my tightly held desire was to be exactly at this point.

I had my marketing degree, and some cash, and a car. And no obligations after the migratory birds left town. Back at seventeen, that was the entire list of what I'd wanted for my next adventure. There wasn't a thing pending on my take-care-of-this list. No person relying on my presence.

For the first time in my life, I was free. No responsibilities to hold me in place, no greater needs tugging me away from exploring wherever I chose.

As our Hyfrydol came to a close and Karl did that thing where he rested back on his heels and closed his eyes while the last beat of music echoed down the nave, I made myself a promise. Before the end of this commitment to the handbells, I'd concoct plans for the next part of my journey.

During the sermon, while the priest was interpreting gospel, Cole caught my eye from the pew overflowing with my family. And the smirk was in full force, which probably meant my face was full of some kind of message that echoed the liturgy's message of making preparations and being ready for travel.

Then his eyes went comic-wide and he bounced his gaze between me and, it turned out, Karl, who was watching our interaction.

Right. The guy who I was supposed to pay attention to, no matter how many personal flaws he harbored. I smirked right back at Cole and rose with the rest of the ringers to perform *Prepare the Royal Highway*. One more song to go for this first Sunday of Advent, and I'd be down to only six more days I was obliged to listen to, of all people, Karl Moore.

FOUR

KARL

So that's why I kept looking at Margo.

It wasn't the streak of orange hair tucked behind her ear, flashing at me every time she glanced down to count notes. And it wasn't that she was so striking, with her heart-shaped face and regal air. Or how she was so swift and sure in her actions, but somehow managed to make each one smooth and deliberate.

I should have figured the way she stole my focus was only about the niggling sense of familiarity that went beyond kinda remembering her from when she was a teen. And then she held a non-verbal conversation with a congregant, and I followed her gaze, and saw the pew full of her lookalikes.

When St. Luke's hired me as their music director, I'd returned to Rockport intending to stay and make it my permanent home. To cut out all the time on the road, going from gig to conference to performance. Combine my work at the church with some teaching and the mixing and recording I could do from my place, so I didn't have to live out of my duffle bag. So I could buy a condo and adopt a dog and set myself up for the life I envisioned.

I'd done all that. Well, not the parts that involved family, but everything else. And as I'd settled in, I'd aimed to get to know St. Luke's regulars. But between virtual events and masks and spacing, I mostly just knew the congregants who were in my choirs, or on the Church Council. I had my back to the pews more often than not during services, but looking at Margo's family now, I should have figured she was one of them. Her siblings, and the men who had to be her dad and uncle, all had the dark hair and dark eyes and steady set to their shoulders.

She put those shoulders to work, damping the last tones of the song. I nodded as my hands dropped back to rest, not just at Margo, but as a signal to the whole handbell choir they'd done a lovely job.

As soon as we'd all returned to the parish house, I sought her out. And, wow. There was nothing immature about the woman framed in the arched window of the choir room, like some sort of stained glass goddess come to life. On top of whatever other changes she'd been through in the past seven or so years, Margo now wore a fierce, combative expression I'd bet I'd never seen before.

Like she could banish anyone in her way. Most of my memories of working at St. Pat's centered on figuring out how to balance the job duties with everything else in my life, and how to learn all the non-music parts of the job in the first place. Admin and facilities management and budgeting, all that. Not what kinds of glares members of the choir sent my way.

The past. It was all the past, and in the present, I had a musician I needed to find accord with, or my new handbell choir would collapse.

"Will you … Margo, can we?" I looked around. The choir rehearsal room wasn't close to being empty, but there were clusters of people who had stashed their music and robes and were only standing around chatting before making their way to the courtyard for coffee and more chat. "Do you mind hanging out for a few minutes? I want to talk to you, but maybe in private. We could go down to the beach for a coffee? My treat, of course."

She looked at me for such a long time I was tempted to fill the silence, despite all my training in the value of letting silence do its work. I held my space while she contemplated me.

When she nodded, I released a breath. It surprised me with how deeply relieved I sounded, and I hastily turned my sigh into a low whistle. A perplexed look flew across her face until she spotted Parsley trotting towards me. My sweet girl sat attentively up against my left side, and I introduced her to Margo. "This is Parsley. Do you mind if she joins us? That is, unless you have a thing against dogs."

She was already reaching to let the golden retriever sniff the back of her hand, and an ember of warmth settled in my chest. I set it aside. I had singers to usher away, an escape to navigate, and approximately seven minutes to dredge up the words I hoped might clear the air.

As soon as was reasonable, I clipped on Parsley's leash and collected Margo. We bypassed the main courtyard, so I wouldn't be caught up conversing with congregants. It was something I normally didn't mind including in my job duties. But I wasn't in the frame of mind for that, not when the past tolled like a handbell someone had failed to damp, long after the song was over.

It was a still day, a touch of damp in the air but clear skies over the Gulf of Mexico as we walked from St. Luke's to one of the grassy esplanades overlooking the water. Semaphore Coffee was little more than a hut with a small deck, but a row of public seating fanned out along the shoreline. As we approached, Parsley checked in with me. I nodded, handing over her leash. She took it gently in her mouth and trotted to our favorite bench. As she settled down, Margo gave me an assessing look, and I wondered if she was judging us for choosing the spot farthest from everyone else.

As if it mattered if this vivacious, staunch woman recognized me for the lonely creature I was. We weren't there for me to impress her, just to be sure we could work together. I offered a polite smile. "What will you have? They do a nice cappuccino here."

She shook her head, and once again I was captivated by that single orange streak in her hair.

"I don't drink coffee. Any kind of tea is fine, but green if they have it."

I admired that, how she was totally confident in her choice, with no need to apologize. Not that disliking coffee was anything to apologize over. Just, the way niceties could shade into self-effacement were often so ingrained, and I liked seeing how Margo bypassed all that.

Speaking of needed apologies. Time for me to make mine. I brought our drinks to the bench.

"Here you go, green tea." I slipped one of Semaphore's baked dog treats to Parsley and sat beside Margo.

"Thanks."

"It's nothing. Listen, I know you never answered my email, and you left a little fast after rehearsal."

She snorted. "Yeah, well. I had to race home to yell at my brother for signing me up without even checking first who'd be conducting."

"You … didn't know it was me? Wait, you didn't even sign yourself up?"

Margo pressed her lips together, then sighed. "Cole, that's my brother, he's got some fixed idea about me needing to reconnect to my faith or some nonsense. So he went and filled out your form without telling me. Don't worry, he knew all the right details. I'm not ringing under false pretenses."

"No, it's not that. You're obviously skilled and we're very glad to have you." I took a tongue-scalding sip of cappuccino. "I do wish I knew before that you'd be surprised it was me. When I saw you sign up, I wanted to talk about what happened back then, but I also thought you volunteering to be in my choir meant I could finally …"

"Finally what?" Maybe she didn't mean to sound so curious. Maybe it was the wind playing with her words, the gulls soaring off with her intent.

"Finally tell you how impressed I've always been by how you acted when you left St. Pat's."

CHAPTER
FIVE
MARGO

I avoided doing a spit take all over his dog. "Excuse me?"

Karl's attention, all focused on me, was too much. I needed a full ensemble around me so he would look away, but we were surrounded only by sand and birds and a super sweet Golden Retriever. He kept his eyes on my face. "It was brave of you, Margo. I meant to tell you at the time, but you never came back to the choir, and I didn't want to intrude. But in leaving, you stood up for yourself. You're a brave woman, and I want you to know how much I admire that."

He almost sounded like he meant it. Like he hadn't frozen there, listening to Father James spewing hateful words about me. Not pushing back, not exhibiting a shred of tolerance or acceptance towards me. Like he hadn't been a part of the problem.

Hadn't he been?

"I was running away, not standing up for myself." I *stand up for myself now.* I'd spent years reinforcing my skills in that area. But back then? It was all fear and instinct.

Karl shook his head. "That's not what I saw. I saw you stand up tall, I saw you rejecting Father James's vitriol. You walked away and it stopped him in his tracks. Your family, too, though I didn't see that part. People told me. I was—"

"You were what?" I interrupted, my voice hard. Screw his revisionist history in the making—I wasn't making time for that. And if it meant my handbell days were over, so be it. "You were right there, witness to everything. Letting him go on. My memories of that day are heightened, okay? And one of them is how you looked away from me when I had to pass you."

He sank against the bench. "You think I was part of the problem."

If he wanted absolution, he was going to have to do more than buy me a cup of tea and offer some platitudes. "You're claiming you're not? I mean, you were an important part of the church. A leader. Maybe you didn't know exactly how he was going to target me, but you still chose silence. Chose looking away."

Every single adult I'd respected—not the ones in my family, but the ones I'd chosen to look up to—failed me that day. And none had ever made the slightest attempt to apologize.

"Margo." Karl's voice wavered a bit. He set his coffee on the bench and swiveled to face me. "I'm glad you walked away. I'm sorry you needed to; I'm sorry your privacy was violated. And I'm sorry you feel—no. No qualifiers. I'm sorry I looked away when I could have chosen to actively support you."

I narrowed my eyes. His words were nice enough, but his actions still rang out loud. "So why did you?"

"I don't claim it excuses how everyone at St. Pat's let

you down. But my youth choir was erupting into a melee, and I had to break it up."

"A melee?" What kind of old-fashioned nonsense was he shoving at me?

"Your friend Ingrid never told you? She knocked your, I guess he was your ex, knocked his whole chair over. He grabbed some others on the way down, and it was turning into a mess." He laughed a beat. "Only time in my life I've had to break up a brawl."

"Ingrid did what?"

"Shoved his shoulders at the same time she hooked a foot on the chair leg to tip it over. I don't even think she expected it to be such an effective move. But, yeah. That's what pulled my attention. I thought you'd known that part, at least."

I stopped shaking my head. "We weren't friends. Me and Ingrid, it was very typical and juvenile, I'm sure. Sweet to each other's faces, but all along rivals to be the best church girl in the parish. If she went after Garrett, it wasn't because she was defending my right to privacy." Even if I was misinterpreting, I knew full well that Ingrid was one of the ringleaders scorching the earth of my whole social world after everyone knew about my abortion.

"Well, whatever her reasons, it distracted me. And I'm sorry. You deserved better witnesses to your courage. It inspired me at the time, which I'm sorry to say I sorely needed that push. And it's been a touchstone of sorts since."

I looked at him. His somber choirmaster clothes matched his serious face, though a hint of a smile lifted his eyes. Like he really was unburdening himself somewhat.

"Okay. Fine, you're not as complicit as I thought. What

happened after the fight that you thought I might not know?"

"Right. So, you left the church right away, which was the right choice. My own path—Margo, it wasn't so tidy. That moment with Father James wasn't the first one I objected to, but I was an employee. It was my first steady job out of college, and my wife and I ... well, it was different. Every little moment, I talked myself out of reacting from an emotional place. I thought if I kept my head down, didn't rock the boat, maybe I could coast along with the music. But when he went from what—I called it old-fashioned rhetoric, but that's another excuse. And then when he was actively hurting a vulnerable congregant—"

"I wasn't vulnerable."

"Margo. Weren't you seventeen? I know that's not infancy, but it's still underage. Father James—me, too, all of us—had a duty of care, even if you'd been an adult. But you weren't. You were young, and your privacy was violated to further his agenda, and I was furious."

I swallowed, trying not to shake from anger but failing. "You? You were furious? My privacy, Karl. My ex spilling our situation—after refusing to help pay for my abortion, by the way. All of my friends turning their backs on me. But you were furious?"

Karl shifted on the bench. "Sorry. You're right. I'm not claiming I acted heroically or anything, but, yeah, I was mad it happened. That anger of mine, it's what got me unstuck about St. Pat's. I typed up all my notes about Father James and sent them to the Bishop, along with my resignation."

I watched the waves retreating from the shore. "So, what? You're saying you did the right thing, eventually?"

Karl looked away for a moment, then back at me with a

determined frown. "I know I handled it badly. I let you down in the moment, and that was about more than you. It was a signal to the rest of the youth choir. To the rest of the congregation. And on top of that, if I'd lifted my head earlier, maybe Father James would have rethought his attack on you. Maybe that would have saved you from the loss of faith you and your brother talked about."

"You think it would have been better to make Father James hide his agenda?"

He spent a little time scratching his dog's silky head. "No. I don't think that. But still: I should have pushed back more. I don't think I could have stopped him speaking out against abortion eventually, if not right then. No matter what the Bishop told him at the time, and I have my doubts he came down hard at all, I'm sure he's made his views clear. Particularly during recent days."

That, we agreed on. "He's hardly the only priest doing that. The Catholic Church has been funding anti-abortion efforts all over the States. I mean, that's an evergreen state-ment, but it's ramped up this past couple of years. Or been more visible, to me, anyway."

"No, I know that. I'm glad to be gone from there." His smile was fleeting, barely a quirk of his cheek and then gone. "I've got my own issues with organized religion, but one of the reasons I like St. Luke's is their inclusiveness. Their philosophy is that scope of God's love is as wide as the ocean. It's a lot more joyous for me to lift voices to the heavens when those voices embrace all the people. I hope your family enjoys attending. I wish I'd realized earlier who they were."

"You didn't remember them?" Sometimes it seemed the whole of Rockport could take one look at any of us and know which family we belonged to. Much as Mama imbued each of us with her values, none of us looked like anyone but Dad and Uncle Bill.

His laugh was a little wry. "Not until I saw the resemblance today. After I resigned, I bounced around a bit. I didn't settle down in Rockport until I came to St. Luke's, and didn't go in there expecting to find anyone I already knew. But if I'd made the connection, I hope I'd have managed to get in touch with you earlier. You deserved to know that not everyone at St. Pat's had vilified you. You took such immediate action, and were so bold and sure. It's something I think about often."

I sat there for a moment, absorbing what he'd said. It wasn't like he was responsible for Father James's screed. I guess I'd always known that, even when it was easier to dismiss everyone in the Catholic Church in one fell swoop. One thing I lost, along with my faith, was my desire to apply any nuance to the people of St. Patrick's.

But it did feel a little good to know that by storming out, I'd helped this man address his concerns about the institution he'd been a part of. I lifted my chin. "Okay."

Karl searched my face. "Okay?"

I cradled my cooling tea cup to my chest and nodded. "Okay. Your apology is accepted. And I appreciate your explanation, for what it's worth."

"You're welcome, Margo." He sounded relieved, and Parsley slumped against him in what looked like doggy contentment.

We sat there for a bit, not speaking, letting the silence between us fill with the shush of waves and the cries of seabirds. It was a beautiful winter's day, and I found myself grateful for it. Grateful for this moment of peace, even if it was tinged with residual bitterness against the Catholic Church.

Finally Karl stirred and said he should get going.

"I'll walk with you." We stood and composted our cups.

We made our way along the path towards the church in silence, his dog trotting happily at his heels. As we approached the turnoff towards his place, Karl turned to me.

"Thank you for hearing me out." He hesitated, then added, "I didn't realize how much I needed that."

I just nodded.

"So. If I'm not making too big a leap, I hope you know I'm not as reprehensible as you'd thought, all these years. Does this mean I get to make you a permanent member of our handbell choir?"

He spoke all light and teasing, but it felt like he was putting more intent behind the question than it held on the surface. He'd edged closer to me on the sidewalk. Or maybe I'd been the one to fix it so our arms brushed against each other as we walked. Either way, his spice-dark scent hit my nose, and I was noticing details like his faint crow's feet and the way his brow was washed smooth in the afternoon sun.

I stopped walking. "Sorry, no. If Cole didn't put that detail on my application, he should have. I'm leaving Rockport soon after Christmas. Once Advent is over, I'm retiring my ringer's gloves."

He nodded slowly, but his eyes sparked with something a little hot, and not at all placid. "No worries. I understand. Thanks again for hearing me out, Margo. See you at rehearsal." He turned and followed his dog towards home, his long, confident stride somehow managing to vex me even as I told myself there was no reason to spend even a minute over-analyzing that final exchange.

SIX

KARL

I'd been to the antique shoppe, which turned out to be code for dusty junk, and two gift stores—both too full of seashell-themed home decor and other such touristy options—and was approaching a jewelers, when Margo barreled out of the salon next door to it. She looked around, distracted, and double-took to focus on me with widened eyes.

"Margo, hi. Hey. What's happening?"

Her expression firmed, lips pressing together. "Rockport," she said, shaking her head.

I raised my brows. That calm confidence of hers seemed shaken. Has it been a facade, how implacable she'd been when we spoke a couple days earlier?

She'd also been alluring, and that hadn't changed. Her casual shorts and sweatshirt look reinforced how she was comfortable in her own skin—or how she had been, before this skittish moment. "Are you fleeing the scene?"

She looked back over her shoulder at the salon, tucking her streak of orange hair behind her ear. "Basically, yes."

"Why?" I asked. "And do you need help?"

Margo sighed, rubbing her temples briefly. "Ingrid," she said. "I went in hoping to refresh my color. Turns out, she works in there."

Oh. I touched her elbow and nodded at the jewelry store. "Want to step in here with me?"

She raised her brows, but followed me in. The place had six or seven showcases of mostly silver jewelry, and I spotted a number of little starfish dangles, and chains like cresting waves, and a pair of earrings shaped like fishing hooks. I blew out an aggrieved breath.

"You mad at the jewelry?"

I waved a polite hand at the store clerk and moved to the back corner, away from him and from the door. "I'm shopping for a Christmas gift for my mother. She doesn't like anything nautical. Which makes you wonder how she's managed to live in Corpus Christi all her life, but it's not the only thing I wonder about her, so. At least I know how to avoid that particular pitfall."

Margo huffed a little laugh, and the air between us settled, like we'd both, just then, managed to relax.

"Are you in a hurry to get her gift? Because, not to get too local tour guide on you, Rockport's monthly Market Day is coming up in a couple of weeks. There's bound to be something there without any scales or—would those abalone turtles be too oceanic?"

Leaning down, I peeked at the bracelet she was indicating. "Afraid so. And yeah, I need to get the gifts in the mail soon or I'll hear something about poor planning. Or ingratitude. Or, I don't know what."

She straightened. "In the mail?"

I looked off, into the next case. As Margo now knew, my parents lived less than fifty miles away. So did my siblings. Picking Rockport as home meant we'd be close, but not expected to spend a ton of time together. They wouldn't be able to fail at any expectations my rackety heart would go and set, despite my telling it not to. Including the expectation that I'd be invited for Christmas, instead of them announcing they were all hitting the road for my youngest sister's basketball tournament.

I deflected like a pro. "Maybe these, with the flowers? They don't remind you of the beach, do they?"

Margo eyed me for a bit, then looked at the dangly earrings I'd pointed out. She shook her head, and that orange streak of hair went flying again. I planted my feet to stop myself from tilting towards her to touch it.

"They remind me of spring in the Hill Country."

A handful of words, in her definitive tone, and a tension I hadn't noticed creeping up my spine receded. She evoked fields of bluebonnets and buttercups, and warm days just verging on too hot, and wide blue skies. It felt like a lifeline, after an hour spent sinking further and further into murky thoughts about my family and the holidays.

"They do. I'll get them." But before calling over for help, I tilted my head towards outside. "Do you want to talk about any of that? About Ingrid?"

Margo was drawing in a breath like she'd make quite a statement, when Ingrid herself walked in. I didn't recognize her, but she was wearing a branded salon t-shirt and ostentatiously playing with her cross necklace. Also, Margo stiffened and took a step forward, not even a little focused on me anymore.

"Hey, Jack. Can I take a look at your engraving book again? I'm second-guessing myself about the style for my little Helena's first holy communion bracelet."

I did some mental math, and Margo must have, too, from the raised eyebrows she shot me. Not that I had an issue with teen moms, but it was all wrapped up pretty close to the timing of Margo's departure from St. Pat's, for Ingrid to have a child of communion age.

Instead of approaching the clerk, Ingrid swiveled real slow to face us. "Why, Margo Dunway. Can that really be you? I thought I saw you pass on by, but it hardly seemed possible, not with how you haven't shown your face in town in so long."

Bless her heart, Ingrid was really trying to play the holiest woman in Rockport. Before either of us had a half-second to reply, she planted one hand on a showcase and the other on her heart. "Is that—Mr. Moore?" For the first time, her voice held a note of genuine emotion, and it was a mixture of surprise and ... not glee, exactly, but a definite promise that she would be sharing this encounter with a whole community. She looked at the jewelry in the cases behind us. "What are y'all doing here?"

"Shopping for my mom's present." I said it probably too fast, what with my mind leaping to images of Ingrid telling the whole town Margo and I had been ring shopping. I forced my tongue to not trip as I clarified. "That is, I'm picking out earrings for my mom. And Margo and I ran into each other. Jack, can I get these? Do you gift wrap?"

The clerk brought his keys and his card reader and a gift box over to where I was now stuck, dealing with the transaction. It wasn't quite the Rowan Atkinson scene from *Love, Actually*, but every time I glanced between Ingrid and Jack, I felt a little of the pressure Alan Rickman's character must have felt as his character's covert gift was wrapped. For different reasons, but having to pick one of three holiday-themed bows nearly broke me.

Margo, though. She wasn't even a little crumbled in the face of Ingrid's obvious speculation and delight.

"I'm sure you've wondered about all the ways I've lived a great life since we left high school, Ingrid," Margo said, in a tone that somehow managed to be both bored and amused. "But I really don't have time to catch up now. I'm sure you understand."

She tilted her head down just enough to give Ingrid a long, slow blink, and then she turned back to me. "That looks festive. Your mom's going to love it."

Ingrid's mouth worked, but before she said anything else, Margo had taken my arm and was steering me towards the door.

"Want to get a drink?"

I blinked at the fading light around us, and at Karl. "Sorry?"

"I mean, not coffee—tea, rather—this time. Want to grab a beer or something?"

I was still holding Karl's arm like we'd linked up on purpose, but now he was the one directing our traffic.

I must have nodded, because Karl led me to what he claimed as his favorite bar. It was a dive, but in a charming way. Even more 'everyone knows your name' than usual for this nosy-ass town. He greeted several people as we ordered longnecks and made our way to a booth in the back.

I took a long swallow from my beer. Setting the bottle down on the table, I cast around for something innocuous to talk about. We'd barely begun to know each other again since I returned to town, and somehow we kept diving into these heavy topics. My abortion and subsequent loss of faith. His troubles with his family. That encounter with Ingrid. "So."

Karl sipped his beer. I noticed his Adam's apple bob

slowly. "So." He tried to fight it, but his lips curved into a smile.

I waved my hand. "I guess we've kind of covered the deep end already."

"It's not that I can't do small talk. I just seem to keep missing that step with you."

I scrunched my nose at him. It was weird, being almost comfortable revisiting those tough moments, but not having any banter to fall back on. After a bit, I asked, "Do you like what you do?"

He nodded. "It pays the bills. Well, some of the bills. But yeah, I've always loved working with choirs, and the people at St. Luke's are easy. Most of them. One of the Graces, once we're sitting with the Church Council, you'd never know she was capable of taking direction from me."

I could guess which one. I snort-laughed, and we both sank a little deeper into our seats.

"What about you? Are you working while you're in town? Or is this an extended family visit?"

"It's both. My dad's brother has a hotel here, and needed someone with experience during the high season, for office and front desk work."

"Hence the Market Day advice."

"Hence, indeed. Right before Thanksgiving, I finished a contract job in Austin—that's where I live. Or where I lived? It's all in flux. Either way, I finished that job and Uncle Bill asked me to hire on, so here I am."

Karl played with the label on his bottle as he listened to me, only looking up when another local clapped him on the shoulder in passing. It was a little funny, how many people kept greeting him while he barely looked around the place for familiar faces.

"So, what's next for you?" he asked, when I stopped short of laying out my life plans.

I shrugged as best I could with one shoulder against the wall. "I always figured, since I first left Rockport, I'd get my marketing degree and make a career out of that. Make it so I got to travel while I climb some kind of career ladder. Turn myself into a city person. Pictured myself as one of those people who looks like a professional, but with a unique sense of style. I know that's amorphous, but it was the original idea. And then I graduated in a pandemic, and the company I'd interned at the previous summer said, instead of the full time job I had lined up, they had to take me on as contract labor. So it was working from my bedroom instead of racking up frequent flyer miles, and my brother my only real companion instead of a metropolis full of young strivers. I've been jumping from contract to contract for two years now, and never once set foot in anything like an office until the cramped little room behind the reception desk at Uncle Bill's hotel."

I checked in on Karl to see if he'd glazed over at my monologue. He nodded like it all made sense. Like he'd heard every nuance even with the bar's background noise and holiday tunes playlist. "And that's why you're not staying once tourist season is over?"

"As soon as those birds fly south, I'm doing the same. Well, not flying south. Probably. I don't have my next job lined up, and I don't know where I'll be. But I do know I'll be gone from here."

"Any direction where you won't run into Ingrid on the street?" He was looking up at me again, leaning forward just a little bit. His eyes were warm even in the low light of the bar, and his intent gaze said he got it. Said he understood the deepest truth of me.

He got that it wasn't just Ingrid, or any of her cohort—all of whom probably had heard by now about the salon and jewelry store incidents. It wasn't just the churches or the cramped hotel office or the overwhelming smallness of Rockport.

It was years of feeling I hadn't found my place. Hadn't even gotten to start looking. Years of yearning for new walls, new vistas, new challenges. I didn't want to settle into anything; I wanted to explore everything. It was, finally, my turn.

I smiled into the pleasure of being seen. "Any direction but here," I said, decisive. Like someone who's never doubted herself. "And speaking of directions. I wasn't paying too much attention before. Which way did we come from?"

Karl stood with me. "I'll walk you. You're parked near the salon?"

I grabbed my bag and nodded. "Yep. Thanks."

I tugged down my sleeves against the cool night as we left. And something that wasn't the December air softened at the sight of Karl standing beside me, hair haloed in the streetlamp's light.

"Did I thank you for getting me away from Ingrid earlier?"

He chuckled. "Pretty sure you were the one who got us away. My head was still spinning from the shopping and all."

"Well, maybe. What I noticed was you intervening when I was shaken from seeing her with no warning. Plus, now I have to find a new place to do my hair, and that salon had the best reviews. It was nice you stood up for me. It gave me time to regroup."

"And then you were more than ready to stand up for

yourself." His voice held admiration, and kindness, and that bit of warmth that always rang true. "As you always seem to manage, no matter the circumstances."

It was a rosy view of my life, but maybe not entirely wrong. I'd have to sit with that feeling and decide how much I should own it.

But not just yet. Not when we were approaching my car, and Karl put a hand on my elbow to guide me across the street, and the goosebumps on my legs seemed to come from anticipation instead of the temperature.

I drew us to a halt. "So, it was great running into you."

He grinned, a flash of white teeth in the dusky air. "It's always a festival when I'm around."

I licked my lips. "You know," I said, "I don't think we ever properly finished our last conversation."

He cocked his head to the side, eyebrows raised in question.

"We didn't talk about how you asked me out." I stepped closer, close enough that I could feel the heat emanating from his body.

His voice was low and a little raspy. "Did I ask you out? I thought I only asked about the handbell choir."

"It was implied."

His smile returned, wider than before. "How very forward of me. Did you imply an answer?"

Instead of speaking, I pressed my lips to his. He made a little sound of surprise, but then he leaned in and kissed me back, slow and sweet. His lips were cool and firm against mine. His taste, hops and spice, rooted me in place like my legs were suddenly piers sunk deep into underwater strata. My head was spinning when we separated, and he looked as dazed as I felt.

He spoke quietly. "So if there was a question, I guess that was a yes?"

"Yes."

Another slow smile, and his hands running gently up my arms. "I'm glad. I think we're both glad. But it's ... we've had a lot happen, a lot come up between us in just this week. I'm not trying to move slow, not with you leaving next month, so don't think that's what I'm saying."

My kiss-buzz was fading faster than my beer-buzz. The man needed to stop talking caution. "What are you saying, then?"

Now it was his turn to close the distance between us, kiss me until my lips were tingling. His touch was firm and warm, hands cupping my face, thumbs brushing along my cheekbones. I shivered as he pulled away and gazed at me like I was hidden treasure.

"I'm saying, I want to make sure we have our heads on straight." He threaded his fingers through mine and lifted my hand, bringing it to his lips. My breath caught at the sudden intimacy of it all. Our hands, pressed together. His lips on my skin, and his banked-fire eyes locked on mine. "Can we take just a beat? Talk on Thursday, and go from there?"

Damn him for his deliberateness, when I'd just gotten done expressing my need to fly. But also, damn that part of me trying to banish a bad encounter with a good one. And damn the knowledge I'd fly higher if I reckoned with the bad instead of banishing it.

I squeezed Karl's hand. Brought those long deft fingers to my lips for a quick kiss. "Thursday."

He stood in the parking lot, hands in his pockets and a renewed tilt to his head, watching me as I drove away.

CHAPTER

EIGHT

KARL

I showed up an hour early for Thursday's handbell rehearsal. Not because setting up the tables and pads and bells took so much time. Not because I had much office work to take care of before we got started. I couldn't even blame it on a recovering Parsley's need to curtail the long walk we often took before heading into the parish house.

I vibrated with my desire to see Margo.

The woman intrigued me. I couldn't say if she was much different from when she was a teen, cause all I really remembered about her back then was how deeply she'd impressed me on her way out St. Pat's door. But I'd done the math, and that had been seven years back, making Margo twenty-four.

I'd flung myself into marriage at twenty-two. A decade ago, I'd been convinced I was adult enough to make a life-long decision. Positive my ex and I could manage, together, any growing up either of us still needed. Turned out we did need to mature, but we didn't do it together. I'd been divorced almost as long as I'd been married. I understood

46

now how I'd been clinging to the illusion of stability I thought marriage would be. If my parents weren't interested in giving their oddball son a safe harbor, I could just make my own, right?

Not right.

But Margo didn't seem as foolishly young as I had. Her self-possession and determination and the way she held her head high; I hadn't embodied any of those qualities at her age.

I knew Margo wasn't in Rockport for good. I'd looked back at her application and she—or, rather, Cole—specified she was only available throughout Advent, not that I needed the corroboration. I only pulled it up because I was adding the new players to my contacts.

In case of handbell-related emergencies.

When she arrived, she was nine minutes early. The Graces were, too, and others trickled in soon enough, but none of them zapped my heart when they walked in.

Margo did.

Her confident entry threatened to drop me to my knees, as if I were in the presence of something new to worship. Which was ridiculous, given our actual location. She wore leggings and a long sweater with some kind of bird on it. A robin, maybe? Her ponytail almost hid that beguiling orange streak in her dark hair. But there was something about her. Something unearthly, like she might fly away if the winds suited her.

I cleared my throat and stood straighter. "Okay, everyone," I said, clapping once as I mounted my podium. "We'll start with some rhythm warm-ups today."

The Graces weren't wild about my plan for a processional, and while I stopped them from derailing rehearsal with their concerns, my gaze kept returning to Margo. The way she kept my brain fizzing was deeper and wilder than with any of the women I'd dated in recent years. It reminded me too much of the pining daydreams I used to have, when I thought the best life would involve being with someone who understood my love of music. Growing up, home had been full of the chaotic, competing energies of my sporty parents and siblings. I'd dealt with it by hiding my thoughts behind noise-canceling headphones, then escaping into college, and then marriage.

Enough. I wasn't that isolated teen anymore. I pulled my focus back to finishing up rehearsal on time. Arranged rhythm patterns and bell assignments into a processional plan that suited everyone's talents and abilities. Smoothed out the syncopation in *O Come, O Come, Emmanuel*. Reminded the Grace named Matt to please not wear his Chucks on Sunday, cause they very much, contrary to his opinion, clashed with the choristers robes.

Thanked Margo for taking on four-in-hand with only the briefest of refresher lessons.

Offered to let her stay on a bit late if she wanted to practice once everyone else had left.

Her raised eyebrow and smothered smile told me I was completely transparent. But it worked.

When it was just the two of us, I got certifiably awkward. Once I'd tidied up as many things as I could and run out of useful bell-ringing guidance to convey, it ... was just the two of us. And Parsley, napping in her favorite corner. Which didn't do anything to ease me into conversation.

"So. Thanks. For coming back today."

She nodded. "Made a commitment, didn't I?"

I cleared my throat. "Right. Well, I wondered."

"Because we kissed."

A flash of that juvenile passion went straight to my overheated cheeks. "Because we kissed."

"I meant what I said. I'm leaving in January." Her words weren't encouraging, but she took a couple of steps towards me, smiling.

My voice deepened. "I know."

"And yet, here I am."

"Here you are."

Our eyes locked. I swallowed. "Any chance we can kiss again?"

"Even though I'm leaving in January?"

I shook my head, noting once again how quick and sure she was. Every time we talked, even during Sunday's confrontation, she never hesitated. Never stumbled over words like I did, never seemed at a loss. And it wasn't just being skilled at social interactions. We'd gone deeper than I'd have ever guessed, talking about the problems from St. Pat's, and at all times, Margo spoke her truth with conviction and confidence and never a hint of contrition.

And at some point during rehearsal, she'd released her hair. I itched to catch at that orange streak flowing behind her ear. To twist it in my fingers.

I reached towards her, saying, "Even though you're leaving in January, I want to kiss you."

She surged forward, grabbed at my shirt, and pressed her mouth against mine. When I'd first touched her, I'd thought she would be somehow ethereal, but no. I'd been galvanized by that brief press. Now, she was somehow more solid than I could have dreamed, and so very alive in my arms. She kissed me with energy and enthusiasm and, God help me, I couldn't get enough. Her full lips moved against mine, her fists knotted against my chest, and I wanted to keep her forever in my arms.

I slid my hands around the curve of her back and held her to me.

She sucked in a breath. "Okay. This is weird."

I pulled back, reluctant. "What is?"

"We're at church."

I tightened my hold, smiling down at her. Ridiculously proud of the flush across her cheeks and the brightness of her eyes. "You're the one who kissed me."

"It's still weird. I don't think I can make out with you here."

But she didn't move away. She still clung to my shirt. I planted a trail of kisses across her brow and down her cheek. "Well, do you think you could make out with me somewhere else sometime?"

The moment her body softened against mine, I was rejoicing. Maybe I shouldn't have been. Maybe our age difference was too great, or I was setting myself up to be hurt when she left town, or St. Luke's Church Council would get sniffy and my job would end in shambles.

But maybe all that mattered was the joy that suffused me when she said, "I think that's an excellent plan."

NINE

MARGO

Was it an excellent plan? I mean, probably not. It wasn't a well-thought-out one, for damn sure. After reliving our first kiss way too much, I was in danger of flashing sultry looks at him while he conducted. If I let my silly fluttery feelings have a say in the matter.

So instead of giving any part of me a say, I was going fully in on my impulses. And that's how I learned that the thermal shirt that had hugged his pecs during rehearsal was soft like a treasured favorite. And that even without a recent cup of coffee, he still tasted like cinnamon.

And that my prurient teen thoughts about his jeans might not have been so very wrong.

"You want to follow me to my room at the hotel?"

Karl's voice was gruff. "I walked. Parsley."

At her name, the dog flipped from drowsing boneless-ness to perky attention. We both laughed a little. "So, I can't lure you to my place?"

He pressed a smiling kiss to my lips, which only set all those flutters to some kind of dance on the currents around us. "Give me a few to take her out, and you can drive us to mine?"

While he clipped on Parsley's leash, I scrubbed my palms down my thighs. No second-guessing. He knew the parameters, and, besides, my self-appointed mission was to find my passions. Not that a guy was a substitute for a personal passion, but it seemed on the right track for me to explore all this electric joy between us.

Karl took my hand in the dim parking lot. Christmas lights threw an extra-twinkly glow on his face. He tipped his head. Leaned in.

"I want this," he whispered. "Do you?"

I did. I nodded. "So much."

The kiss we shared in the dark was so sweet, it made me shiver. I climbed into the car and waited for him to settle the dog in the back. His directions home were easy enough. I'd grown up in Rockport, after all, and his condo was right off one of the main beach roads.

Soon enough we were inside. I got an impression of serenity and comfort; lots of music and lots of overstuffed furniture, a real retreat from the world. But we bypassed the living area in favor of what I expected to be his bedroom.

I laughed when he shut the door and turned on the light. "What's this?"

The room was crammed with bookcases and armoires and crates full of books and sheet music. An overflowing desk sat under the one window, opposite a futon covered with more blankets than anyone on the Gulf Coast could ever need.

Karl led me there, shoving a quilt aside and drawing me down into a proper little nest of space beside him. "It's my study. It's the only room Parsley isn't allowed in. I thought ..."

Whatever he meant to say, I took as encouragement to launch myself at him again. Before long our legs were entangled as we stretched out on the futon, our kisses interspersed with gasps of breathless pleasure as we discovered each other's sensitivities. The interplay of our hands and tongues and weight and pressure sent a flood of heat to my core. I rocked against his hardness, and, frustrated it wasn't enough, shifted to straddle one firm thigh.

"Margo."

Somehow I managed a light kiss to his cheek, even as I ground down on him. "Karl."

"I want you."

"That," I said, yanking off my shirt, "is damn good news. Does Parsley let you keep condoms in here, or what?"

I groaned when he eased me back, taking control of our movement with his hands at my waist. "Margo," he asked, "are we moving too fast here? I know we said making out, and this ..."

"This is not moving fast enough. Quit wasting time." I undulated to make my point, and he groaned.

"I planned to explore you slowly. I want to do this right."

I grinned, though my breath was coming in pants. "Okay, Mr. Conductor, you know we're not at rehearsal now. We can just ravage each other without all the orchestration."

His eyes glimmered when he smiled. But he stilled the rocking of my hips, like, never mind the erection hard against my core. "I'd like to see you. I'd like to look at you and touch you and kiss you."

"Right back at you." I toyed with the hem of his shirt, scraping my nails under the fabric and salivating at bit at the thought of all that warm skin I'd soon have my mouth on.

Then I remembered I wasn't waiting for his direction, and I unbuttoned his pants. Like that, he had me on my back, and was yanking down my bra straps to release my breasts to his hands.

"Oh, good, yes." I arched into his touch. "Good plan. Like that."

"I adore how you make it look so easy to be you. So comfortable in yourself. Like you don't give a damn what anyone thinks."

"Oh, I do." The words came out readily, and I meant every one of them. "Not everyone, not all the time. But you? I want you to see me. I want you to think I'm sexy. I want your desire. I really, really want you to fuck me."

He groaned, and I thought I was about to get my wish. But instead he dipped his head to suck at my nipple. My skin sizzled. I ground against his thigh again, needing him. He sucked harder. "Karl. Please. Now. Please."

"Shh."

He pulled away and pushed himself to his feet. Slowly, because obviously he knew I love-hated the slowness, he stripped off that soft, soft shirt and revealed all the hard and soft planes of his torso.

In return, I tore off my bra and flung it at him. He smiled, the arrogant jerk, and tucked it in his back pocket. "You better have that condom in your other pocket."

"Patience, Margo. It's not far. But first these." He dropped to his knees in front of me and went for my waistband like slowness was his favorite erotic torture device. Before I could think up a complaint, his thumbs were parting my folds and he was trailing biting kisses up the insides of my thighs.

My hips jerked up in a wave of pleasure. "Oh my God."

"You're beautiful like this." He looked up at me, gaze glazed with lust.

"I'm in agony."

He laughed and nudged my legs wider, and I got the relief I craved. I gasped as he explored every fold of my sex. The way he licked at my clit, the way his fingers delved into my opening, the way his thumb found my tight little nub, slowing and firming the pressure as I directed, drove me over the highest peak of pleasure. My vision darkened. My heart pounded. My chest heaved. I'd flown away to somewhere else entirely, and it took a sec for me to notice Karl again.

He'd lost the pants, and found the condom, and was sitting beside me, legs spread wide, cock jutting, eyes dark and devouring every sweat-slick inch of my skin. And all I could think was I didn't want any slow or sweet or soft or tender. I wanted his cock inside me, filling me, fast and fierce.

I straddled him, almost shocked by my new surge of energy, and rolled protection down his lovely erection. He palmed my thigh and I took him into me, tight and hot and wild, undulating down inch by inch until our bodies were flush.

Karl's face was taut. He closed his eyes and tipped his head back, gasping, "Christ, Margo."

Then I rode him, and all he said was my name, over and over, in a plea, a chant, praise and need and wonder.

"Margo," as he gripped my hip.

"Margo," as he mouthed at my nipple.

"Margo," as his thumb traced the now-familiar circle around my clit.

Right as I came again, gripping handfuls of his hair and saying I don't know what, he flipped us so I was propped back on that nest of blankets. And then there were no other words, just the way he moved in me, hard and fast and deep, like at last he'd figured out about how we should be racing and racing through this fuck, Like he'd realized the sooner we poured all our energy into it, the sooner we could do it again. Like he knew how utterly peaceful it would be, after we came, to lay in the silence, his weight pressed to mine, our hearts beating at each other through our chests.

How we'd be full, and good, and ready for more passion to come our way.

TEN

KARL

"What is the deal with all these blankets?" Margo's voice was breathy and just a touch needy and it popped the very last bubble of reserve I'd been harboring.

After ditching the condom, I rolled to my elbow and looked down at her. Mussed hair and bright eyes and lips wide with passion and with a smile. I swooped down to kiss that delectable mouth. "I record and mix audio in here."

She looked around, clocking, I guess, my equipment and screens and piles of notes. "Oh, right. Sound baffling."

"You know about that?"

"Two of my sisters are married to rock stars."

Huh. So they were. In Rockport, the Dunways were just the Dunways, not a conduit to a world of fame. "And you're not the only musical one in your family, are you? I think one of your sisters sang in my choir back then."

"Larissa, yeah. The oldest. And Sarita and I were in orchestra. Cole in band. Jeannie, she's the one married to Brendan Brody, is the only one with, like, no musical talent at all. Oh, and Emmeline can play piano but doesn't like it." With that, Margo scooched up and dragged one of the lighter blankets across her body. "Never mind them. I need to know. Were you, like, a sex god all this time?"

"I'm not sure I deserve quite that much praise." But since I hadn't covered up when she did, I was sure Margo noticed how my cock jumped at the compliment.

"Sure you do. It's not as common as it should be, for a guy to focus first on getting his partner off. And to do it with unerring skill? Top of the charts, Karl."

I studied her face, looking for signs of bitterness or old hurts or anything along those lines. "You've slept with some serious duds, sounds like."

She laughed and reached up to toy with my hair. "Don't be so grim about it. I'm speaking more from collective experience than personal. If someone I'm with is that selfish or won't take direction, they're not getting a second chance with me."

A whole swirl of bubbles I hadn't realized I was holding back popped, leaving me washed with hope. "Yeah? Does that mean second chances are on the table for me?"

"Oh, I think so." Margo's smile was lazy and satisfied. "I'm thinking you and I could have a lot of fun together."

"Agreed." My own smile was uncivilized and uncontainable. I drew my fingers across her collarbones and into the shadowed territory between her breasts, not quite displacing the blanket.

She shivered and relaxed into the futon, tracing the lines of my face as she lifted her chin slightly. "I like these."

"My crow's feet? Why, cause you like the reminder of how I'm ancient compared to you?"

"Come on. We're both adults. How old are you?"

"Thirty-two."

"Hardly decrepit. That's, what, eight years? Larissa is older than you." Her knees angled up, letting the blanket pool around her waist. "Besides, you seem to have plenty of stamina from where I'm laying."

My growing erection seemed to agree. The curves of her hips and thighs and ass taunted me, but I hadn't yet gotten as much time with her breasts as I'd like. I kept tracing the not-quite-exposed flesh of her chest, and soon Margo was writhing and arching her spine enough for the blanket to slip, slip, slip down until one breast popped free. It was manna to a starving man, and I swooped to envelop her nipple in my feasting mouth.

"Oh, God." Margo's hands gripped my shoulders tighter. "That's, fuck, that's so good."

She was right. The simple pull and swirl of my tongue around her hardening nipple sent shudders through her frame and made me want more. Wanted every twist of her body in response to my touch. Her skin felt like satin, so smooth and fine under my fingertips and lips, and I wanted to lap it all up. Her whole body undulated beneath me and it was an utter tease to my dick, which I needed to bury inside her while her body writhed around me.

I stood and tugged her to her feet.

"No, wait. What are you doing?"

"I have to fuck you, Margo."

"What you have to do is suck on my other breast. This lopsided attention thing is bullshit."

I dragged her into my arms, and the impact of all our naked skin meeting was bliss. "I'm not going to neglect it, sweetheart. I couldn't. Your breasts are a gift, and I'm going to treasure them, just like I did your clit and your cunt. I'm going to trace their heft and pinch their tight nipples and devour them while you tell me exactly how skilled I am at reading your body's responses. While you beg me for more, because I'm setting all your nerves on fire. But while I'm do all that, you're going to keep getting hotter and wetter and more desperate for me, okay?"

Her eyes were blown wide, and she nodded, breathing fast.

"But the rest of my condoms are in my bedroom, and when I've got you so hot and so wet and so desperate, I'm going to have to fuck you. I have to bury myself in you and feel just how much you need me there. How your body grips and clings while I thrust, and thrust, and drive us both closer and closer to the edge. Do you agree?"

She answered me with a kiss, and it wasn't everything I needed from her, but it was damn close. Intent and sensual and eager and us. Me and Margo.

I led us to the bedroom, skirting past Parsley who got the message with a quick word to keep hanging out in the living room. Margo crawled up my bed and watched me retrieve the box of condoms, teasing me all the while with her splayed legs and exploring fingers. There was nothing like watching a woman show me how she liked to be touched.

"You're taking too long. I warned you about the lopsided thing, Karl."

In response, I found the lube in my bedside drawer and set it beside her.

And then I made good on every dirty promise I'd made, and it was better than I could have dreamed. When we collapsed back on my rumpled and sweaty sheets, I reached to capture her hand.

"Thanks."

"Right back at you, mister. You talk a good game and I'm not mad about your execution."

"Well, you were complaining a lot. I had to mitigate that."

She squeezed my fingers. "God, you're not going to turn out to be a comedian dude, are you? Cause those second chances aren't only about your skill in bed."

"Dire threats." I looked at her. "If that didn't count as my second chance, can I officially ask for that now? Do you want to spend the night?"

Her brow pinched for just a sec before she hid her expression. "You still remember the part about me leaving next month?"

It shouldn't have stung, being reminded about our time limit. "Yeah, of course. But this was fun. You were officially so right to say we shouldn't waste time. I want more, while you're here and if you're willing."

Her smile didn't fully inhabit her face, not like the ones I'd earned earlier. "Sounds good. Sure. We'll make a plan."

With that, she slid out of bed. When she emerged from my bathroom, her damp hair was tamed down, hiding the orange streak again, and she was fully encased in one of my bath sheets. I'd slipped into clean boxers and a t-shirt and gathered her clothes from the detritus of my study. "Water's there if you want it. How about some food? A beer?"

She dug through the pile for her underwear. "Thanks, no. I'm on shift first thing tomorrow, so it's best I head out now."

"Margo." Something in my voice, or maybe some genuine urge of hers, stopped her fussing around and got her attention on me. I stepped forward and laid one of my business cards on top of her shirt. "That's my cell. There's no need to palm me off with niceties. Maybe I'm not ancient, but I've dated enough since my divorce to understand when I'm getting a polite line. Only call me if you want to call me, but just so you understand? I'm not seeing anyone else right now, and I'm very interested in seeing you again. If you change your mind about those second chances, and want to restrict us to conductor and musician from now on, that's fine. But if you do call, I'm going to have a very long, very detailed list of ways I want us to experience each other, and I'm willing to spend as much time as either of us can spare between now and when you leave exploring them."

She swallowed, looking from the card to my face to my body and back. And she didn't answer me.

But she did drop the towel and took her sweet time covering every enticing inch of skin as I leaned back and watched. Once she was dressed, she tucked my card into her bra and approached.

Maybe it would have been cooler, more mature, to sit back and let her leave. Instead, as soon as she was close enough, I wrapped her in for another long kiss. She responded with sweetness and fire, and it made it a bit easier to watch her walk away, leaving me, once again, alone.

CHAPTER
ELEVEN
MARGO

Uncle Bill's hotel wasn't fancy, but it was very good at being itself. Charm, most people called it. Forty-eight rooms, plus the three for staff. Tasty to-go breakfast boxes for all the birders to grab on their way out the door. A library of bird guides and binoculars and waterproof outerwear for residents to check out. Local artwork in every room; extra towels because if people weren't seeking migratory flocks they were going to the beaches; cool blues and greens throughout.

We'd all worked there, off and on, growing up. Especially Cole and me, when I was repaying Bill for the abortion and we were saving for Cole's top surgery. My favorite gigs were behind the scenes, though everyone had to be customer-facing to some extent. For this winter, Bill had me coordinating tours, taking a few front desk shifts, and updating the website to look a lot less like 2004 got lost in it.

It suited me at least as well as my last job, which had been all remote and too overloaded with Zoom meetings. The firm liked me enough to offer a permanent position as my contract expired, which I felt a bit bad rejecting out of hand. But at least there, no one in my family was pulling out guilt tactics to get me to accept.

Uncle Bill was getting downright ruthless. "Margo, sweet girl, do you know how much the guests are raving about you?" he asked as I opened his office door. He was leaning back in his chair, riffling through a stack of papers. He wasn't wearing his glasses, and I noticed the rings under his eyes. They'd been getting deeper lately, and his smiles a little tighter. "I printed the comments for you."

I laughed. "I can read them online."

"Well, I like having the paper. Maxima gave me an album to paste them in."

"Aunt Max boasted at Thanksgiving about offloading all her old scrapbooking supplies on you. You know she's decluttering."

He deflated a tad, and set down the printouts. "Well. I still like them."

"And I appreciate the kudos."

"Thing is, sweet girl, you're good for this place. And I'm not getting any younger."

"As your gullibility with Maxima proves."

He blew a raspberry at me. "Stop making out like I'm senile. I'm trying to compliment you."

I sat opposite him and gave him my best 'not having it' face. "You're trying to butter me up so I agree to train up and one day take over this place so you and Sam can spend your days scrapbooking or something."

"What if I am?"

"I'm not interested."

"See, you keep saying that, but what if you just don't realize yet that you are? Your dad says you don't have a plan for after migration season. Why not stay here, then?"

I rolled my eyes. "The family's been trying to get me to move home for years. I don't know how many more ways I can tell you to stop ganging up to protect me like I'm a bird with a broken wing."

"Ganging up is a sign of love and family, Margo."

"Is it really love when you try to wear someone down with emotional manipulation?" I asked.

He frowned. "That wasn't what I was doing."

"You were using every trick in the book," I said. "The silly salary you're paying me, the printouts, the 'I'm not getting any younger' card. Come on, Uncle Bill, I'm not falling for it."

"All right, all right," he said, holding up his hands in surrender. "You got me. But that doesn't change the fact that we could really use your help around here. And why not?"

"I don't know. Because it's not my dream?"

"What is your dream, Margo? What is your big plan?"

I didn't have an answer to that.

And the flash I had of Karl's face was no help. I hadn't called him yet. Hadn't decided exactly what I was going to do there. I mean, have more great sex, sure. That's why his number was in my phone before I even pulled away from his curb Thursday.

But fun as he was, Karl wasn't part of my big plan, any more than Uncle Bill's hotel was.

Or more accurately, I didn't have a big plan. Not one that I could point to and say, "That. That's my dream. That's what I want to do with my life."

Not that I needed one. I was twenty-four. Sure, I had peers who knew what they wanted to be, had known for years. And good for them, but that wasn't me. I worked jobs I didn't love while exploring how I wanted my adult life to go. Plenty of people did the same. Nothing wrong with going through the motions, when the motions were my choice.

But now? I chose to search out the things I loved. For my own dream.

Because if I didn't, I knew how easily I might float into a career like the one at the hotel, settle into some Rockport-like place, and maybe even sink into a relationship with someone like Karl.

Whatever my plan was, drifting into someone else's idea for me wasn't it.

"I don't know what my dream is," I told him. "But I'm working on it. Working on it is what I want to do."

"And in the meantime, you're just going to keep saying no to me?"

"Yes," I said. "I am. I'm sorry, Uncle Bill. But no."

He thumbed the printouts and sighed. "Oh, fine. Search for your passion. Maybe I can talk your little sister into taking over my hospitality empire."

I grinned as I stood. "Let her finish college first, though, yeah?"

He made a noncommittal noise as I left. I'd drop a warning to Emmeline when she came back for Christmas break, but meanwhile? I was going back to Project: Journey. Destinations were all well and good, but for me, I had to enjoy getting there.

TWELVE

KARL

Not a word from Margo since Thursday night. I'd kept the phone on me during Friday's meeting with the ministry team, and Saturday morning's rehearsal with the youth choir. Made no difference, because she didn't call.

Parsley nosed sympathetically at me when I changed my dog-related song lyrics to Margo-related ones, but when I tried to leave her behind on the way to church, she gave me the look of the utterly betrayed, so I relented. Even though it would mean asking the Graces, again, to not slip her too many snacks after services.

My dog's company was a good distraction as we walked, and I found myself in full-voice singing, "She rules my house, with goofball grace / And makes the people praise / The glories of her silkiness / And wonders of her nose / And wonders of her nose / And wonders, wonders of her nose."

"Her nose?"

The amused voice was behind me, and I turned fast

without paying attention to Parsley's leash. Fortunately there was enough slack so I didn't fall at Margo's feet.

"Parsley has a very nice nose."

She approached, crouching to let my dog sniff at her and accept some petting. "Well. It's not that I disagree."

"You don't think it's worth singing about?"

Margo stood then, and we were so close together. "It wouldn't have been my first pick, but the bigger problem is how I'm going to ring *Joy to the World* now without laughing." Margo pressed her lips together, then reached to brush her fingers through my hair. It was a tender gesture, full of her usual surety, almost enough for me to forget all the lonely moments of the past few days.

"Hi." I pulled her in for a kiss. It was a cross between the light, laughing ones we'd sometimes shared, and the galvanizing ones where I didn't want to let her go.

"Hi," she replied, then looked around. "Is it time to go in?"

I checked my phone, remembering to put it on silent now I had Margo with me at last. "For me, yes. You're welcome to join me."

"I'd love to."

We held hands as we walked to the parish house, Margo's fingers warm in mine. Her nails were purple now, and I wondered what other little changes I'd find if I got to explore her like I wanted. At the doors, I kissed her again, a little more tentatively as I thought to gauge whether she was ready for everyone to know we were ... whatever the name was for what we were doing, sleeping together and kissing in the open.

I was about to ask, but Margo, of course, was ahead of me. "I never texted, but I'm hoping we can take a walk after services? And maybe your place after? I brought an overnight bag in case the day goes real well."

"I'd love that. Parsley would, too."

She turned to the dog. "Would you, now? Do I have to sing about your nose to earn your company?"

"Not only her nose. There's songs about how she wags her whole butt, and ones for when she's trying to convince me she's starving, and it's been a while, but I think I remember the one for not chewing on every bit of trash she finds on the beach."

I prayed I came across as charming instead of ridiculous, or desperate. The countdown to the new year and the end of our connection was loud in my mind, and there was so much I wanted with this woman. I'd taken it slow, in my other post-divorce relationships, but slow wasn't going to put Margo in my bed for as much of December as possible.

Yeah, I knew diving in head-first—okay, maybe it was dick-first—might to lead to some shattering of my emotions down the line, but I didn't have time to erect a protective wall around my heart. My desire for Margo had knocked me for a loop, sometime between the first green tea at the beach and the last beer in town.

Maybe rehashing all that Father James stuff had stripped away something for me. Something that was too tied up in what a mess I'd once been in, both personally and professionally. A scab over my soul that needed to break away so I could fully heal. And it left me open to pursing something new.

Or maybe Margo was a sexy shock to my system and I couldn't hold back.

To my slight surprise and complete pleasure, Margo waved to the Graces as they wandered in, then wrapped her arms around my neck. I leaned down for a brief, but meaningful, kiss, reveling in the chance to stroke my hands down her back to her waist.

Resisting, cause I'm good like that, the allure of her heart-shaped ass.

I squeezed her to me a second too long, dropping my forehead to hers. "Grab me from the courtyard when you're ready to leave after."

She pressed hers hips into me, a subtle but sexy promise, and smiled.

It settled into me like the peace of the season, and I went into our services carrying a new kind of faith. That of trusting that, somehow, the convictions I'd held onto throughout the sadness of my divorce and the loneliness of making a life for myself since then, was all part of something bigger. Instead of building a wall around my heart, I'd constructed a foundation. One that meant I was ready to create a home alongside someone else.

Was I making the kinds of leaps and bounds that meant I was likely to fall and shatter it all? I knew Margo was leaving. No matter how solid and sure of her place she seemed, standing there amongst my choristers, in a month she'd be gone.

But couldn't it be a good idea to whole-heartedly pursue our desire? To accept the something molto allegro between us that lay outside my normal experience? The relationships I'd had in the past few years were comfortable. Sometimes largo and sometimes andante. A repeating pattern of drinks, dinner, sleep together, da capo al coda. I knew all the beats.

Leaving my comfort zone, even if it meant pain later on, could only teach me more about myself. More about how to share my heart. And those lessons could endure long past the limits Margo had imposed. They could expand my soul, make me ready for the something more I craved.

So being with her, for however short a time, was worthwhile.

It didn't have to mean that when she left, I'd crash into the rubble of my ruined foundations.

THIRTEEN

MARGO

Our walk along the shore ended at a restaurant with lots of outdoor seating. It was the coldest December day yet, but in Rockport that meant we wore light jackets zipped to our throats.

Over burgers and a shared order of fries, Karl told me about Parsley's big accident just before Thanksgiving. Something in me went a little sideways, imagining her hurt. Somehow or another, I'd gotten extremely attached to his very good dog. I hated the idea of her hurting.

Back at his place, we dispensed with chatting and were diving into the fun physical stuff when my phone rang. I winced in apology as I answered.

"Cole. What's wrong?"

"What's wrong with you? You sound breathless."

"I had to rush to grab the phone before it rang out." I wrinkled my nose at Karl, who was picking up our clothes out of Parsley's reach. I wasn't sure what his return look was, cause I was busy patting my heart down into a more normal rhythm.

It's not like every time Cole phoned instead of texted it

was because he sought my support. But transphobic people got to walk the streets like they weren't semi-sentient scum, and sometimes that meant awesome people like my brother had to encounter them. All it had taken was a couple of post-encounter calls for Cole's ringtone to leave me a bit anxious and a lot ready to fight. He'd told me I needed to chill, but my nervous system hadn't gotten the memo. At any rate, this call wasn't a call for help.

"Gogo, listen. I want to talk about a couple things. Are you busy? It's your day off, right?"

I smothered my laugh and sank down to the sofa. Tracing my fingers up and down Karl's inner arm, I asked him, "You okay if I take this?"

He nodded. "Take your time. I'll put the kettle on."

"Why, Margo Adele, what is going on out there?" Cole's voice was all innuendo and intrigue. "Tell me that's not the dulcet tones of one Karl McChoirface Moore."

"Hush up. What are you calling for? And don't tell me it's to interrogate me, because you had no idea until now where I would be spending the night."

Cold flat out chortled. "Gogo girl, you owe me a very long conversation."

"Okay, okay moving on. What's happening there?"

Cole took a deep enough breath that my own lungs constricted. "So, first thing: your sub-letter and I had a chat. She's liking it here so much, she wishes she had the second bedroom so her friend could move in."

I just blinked. "Um?"

"Hear me out, okay? Maybe this choir director you're doing will make the decision a little easier for you, but Margo, listen. I'm leaving."

Now my heart and lungs were churning like they'd been caught in a riptide. "You're what?"

"You remember that job with InFront Advocacy?"

I made some kind of positive noise, just waiting for Cole to continue. He'd mentioned it as the kind of social policy he hoped he could do one day, once he had enough experience, but had brushed me off when I'd suggested he apply. Said he wasn't qualified yet. "You applied?"

His laugh was a little wild. "That's the thing, Gogo. I didn't. They sought me out. I guess Nina knows somebody over there. At some point, she told them about me, and when they were reviewing applications, the HR director remembered me and reached out to Nina to see if I'd be interested."

"Cole, oh my God."

"I know. It's so wild. I've been, like, reviewing the paperwork and trying to get my head around it. There's a relocation package, Margo. Imagine that—they're paying me to move."

He kept talking compensation and benefits and nine thousand other things I was so glad for him about. But ... "Cole?"

He hummed encouragement. He knew me as well as I knew myself, so he knew what was coming.

"When did all this happen?" My voice absolutely did not crack.

After a moment, quietly but firmly, he spoke again. "I needed to do it all myself. Margo. I needed it to be my negotiations, my pro-con list. My decision."

I was nodding, not that he could see me, but it seemed necessary. Like I could convince my hurt and anger to subside and make room for all my happiness for him. "I get it. I do. And I never want to get in the way of your accomplishments. You know that, right? I'm so proud of you. I know you're proud of yourself."

"I am." I could almost see his own nods from the hundreds of miles separating us. "I really am."

"So, good job. When do you start?"

"January third. That's why I want to figure out the sublet as soon as possible."

"Oh right. Okay. Okay, it's great, actually. She can bring in her friend in, then we can see about getting the lease transferred to their names. That way we'll be in the clear when we move."

"Gogo."

I hated the kindness in his voice, but I could only talk about logistics for so long while he tried to interrupt me. I swallowed back my words, and swallowed back my tears while I was at it. I needed him to say it, but it wasn't like I didn't know.

How many times had he told me? "We don't need each other, Gogo." And we both knew he was right. Neither of us was escaping a town full of disapproval anymore. We'd stood up for each other and, in the process, learned to stand up for ourselves.

But, somehow, I never let myself believe that Cole not needing me could mean us living in far different cities.

I took as deep a breath as I could manage, squeezing my eyes shut. "So. January?"

"Listen, you don't even have to come back, if you decide to stay in Rockport. To take Uncle Bill's job or whatever else. I can have the movers send your stuff down there, and we can do the rental paperwork remotely. But, Gogo, I'm moving to Philly on my own. Tell everyone they can buy me scarves and boots for Christmas, cause I'll need all the layers. But I also need to show up in Philly as Cole Dunway, independent man. I need to be in a place where no one's seen my awkward transition beard. And with people I won't be default to leaning on if I get scared. I love you, little sis, but if you're with me, I'm not relying on myself the way I need."

My tears were fully streaming now. Karl set a mug of tea beside me, and a box of tissues, and said something quiet to Parsley.

She hopped up beside me and pressed her weight against my side, licking my hand once, but not in her 'please scratch me immediately because no one has ever before lavished attention on me' way. Karl leaned over to kiss the crown of my head and tilted his head down the hall.

"Gogo? You there?"

I sniffed, then gave in and blew my nose loudly. It wasn't like either Karl or Cole didn't know I was crying. "I'm here."

"Listen, you're going to have to get over your thing of imagining the worst conclusion when I phone, because I'm going to be calling you all the time to just, you know, complain about the dirty snow, or how there's no H-E-B in Pennsylvania."

"Or to tell me about your Gritty sightings."

"And which cheesesteak place really is the best."

"How many tourists are taking Rocky-on-the-steps photos."

"What books I'll find at Giovanni's Room."

"Oh, shit." I blew my nose again. "I can't wait to visit you up there."

"I'm told it stops snowing by the end of March."

Parsley bumped her nose at me, and I obliged by stroking her ears. She wasn't quite content with that, according to her paw on my thigh, so I leveled up to scratching under her collar. "Okay, April first or so, be sure you have my guest bed ready."

"It'll be the same sofa we have now, Margo. If you think I'm leaving that beauty behind for sub-letters …"

"But I like your sofa. Where am I supposed to flop down after dealing with too much traffic?"

"Two words: relocation package. I don't even have to find the movers myself. Say goodbye to the coffee table and the good desk chair, too. If you want, though, I'll leave you that wobbly bookcase."

"I'm hanging up on you now." I didn't want to sulk to Cole about how inconvenient it suddenly was that he'd been the one who'd refurnished our apartment last year. It wasn't his problem to navigate.

"I'm sure you'll find comfort in the arms of some local cutie. Speaking of which, why haven't you shared one hint of this situation with me yet? Last you told me, he was absolved from the sin of disrespecting you, but now you're, what, making him do penance in the bedroom?"

"It's temporary." With any luck, my dismissive tone hid my guilt for not telling him about Karl earlier. I'd definitely had time to share, and I hadn't, and that wasn't anything I cared to examine.

"But is it hot?"

I glanced over my shoulder to the clear coast of an empty hallway. "So goddamn hot. Like you wouldn't believe."

"Hmmm. Well, I won't tell you how to live your life, but he seems like the kind of guy who fixes wobbly bookcases, if you know what I mean. And, Gogo, seriously: it wouldn't be any kind of failure to your life of adventure if you let yourself stay there a while. See what happens."

"Sounds like you're telling me how to live my life, Cole."

He laughed. "Big brother prerogative. Just … think about it, okay?"

We said our goodbyes, and I blew my nose one last time. Parsley sighed and rested her head on my lap. I sipped my perfectly brewed tea. Everything was so comforting, and so easy. It scared the hell out of me, how I risked falling into the ease of things like Bill's job, and this sweet dog, and a thoughtful lover, instead of making decisions for myself.

That wasn't what I wanted at all.

CHAPTER

FOURTEEN

KARL

I overheard enough of Margo's end of the conversation to know she might want space.

She might even want to leave, which, of course. Whatever she needed. Maybe it was a leap on my part, assuming her openly physical affection at church meant a kind of connection. That our easy, open lunch conversation meant she saw me as a confidant. Truth was, I hoped for more.

I hoped she would turn to me for comfort.

I wanted to be the one she came to when she was sad or scared or angry.

I wanted to be the person she sought when she needed someone to just be there, no questions asked.

But that wasn't our situation. We were half-way through Advent, and at a stretch, this could count as a third date. My being patient and willing to listen might not matter, since she wasn't planning on sticking around.

Even if that call from Cole suggested she didn't have as much to return to Austin for as she'd expected.

I got absorbed in mixing a couple of tracks for a freelance job, and was startled when Margo came up behind me. She'd obviously washed her face and straightened up some, but she wasn't wearing her sweater or shoes. I took it as a good sign, which probably beamed through my smile as I turned to her.

"Hey."

"Hey yourself." She tilted her head to the door. "Thanks for the tea."

"Was it okay? I bought a couple of boxes, so if you want something different ..."

She stopped my move towards the kitchen, slipping herself into my lap. "It was great."

Her voice was quiet and her body far from relaxed. I wanted to ask about her troubles, but was wary of pushing too hard. Instead, I wrapped my arms around her and held on tight.

"You're a good person, Karl," she whispered into my chest.

I stroked my hand up and down her back, trying to think of something—anything—to offer comfort. But in the end, all I could do was be there for her. Hope it helped.

"Thank you," she said after a long time, her voice muffled against my shirt. "I needed that."

"Anytime," I told her, meaning it probably too much.

"Ugh. Now I've made an unglamorous mess of myself in two rooms of your house."

I smirked. "If you want to talk mess, didn't you note the state of the bedroom after you left Thursday?"

She pushed against my shoulders. "Wow. I think you're responsible for some of all that."

"And I cleaned it up. Aren't you impressed with me?"

"Did you? Was it arduous?"

"Changing the sheets and buying more lube? So arduous. I deserve medals."

"Definitely. Many medals."

We both smiled a little, and she finally relaxed against me. I took the opportunity to kiss her forehead, and then her nose, before finding her lips. She met me with familiar heat and intent. It wasn't the lazy exploration of before her phone call, but needier, maybe even serious. It was like she was trying to shove every good thing about us into a single moment, to store it up for when we parted.

She was leaving in January.

With those thoughts, my hands darted to her hips, pulling her against me. I used the half-second to pull back from the kiss, just enough to speak. "Can I make a suggestion?"

"Sure."

"Come to bed."

"Good suggestion."

In truth, as so often happened with Margo, it was more of a plea.

I rose to my feet, holding her firmly against my body, and she let me lead her down the hallway. I laid her on the bed and settled beside her.

I let her set the pace, kissing her, touching her, exploring every part of her like I'd been dreaming of. And she did the same with me. It was an intense, almost urgent hour of orgasms and heavy breaths, but also quiet moments of stillness and sweet smiles.

It was exactly what I needed, and I gave her everything I had. I hoped it was enough for now.

I couldn't think about being enough for any longer than now.

Once we'd showered—together, which almost defeated

the point of getting cleaned up—I took us to my favorite taco stand for dinner. Margo tried to talk me into trying her smoked brisket with spinach, but I knew an abomination when I heard it. And once she'd tasted my barbacoa and given me the wide eyes of culinary delight, I went back to order a couple more. Not that the al pastor or grilled shrimp tacos weren't equally worth devouring, but: pleasure in the moment. That was the way Margo was determined to approach life, and I was in no position to dissuade her.

If anything, I should learn from her.

After eating, I steered up towards the tip of our peninsula, near where Copano Bay met Aransas Bay. We climbed out of my truck and settled into the bed, which I'd padded with a bunch of the soundproofing blankets from my study. Looking out in the gathering darkness towards San Jose Island and the Gulf, all we saw was scattered boat lights and emerging stars.

"You're making me feel like a teenager," she said.

My whole body was buzzing with lust and some happy kind of excitement. It took considerable effort to stop touching her and pay attention to her words. "How's that?"

"You know, making out in cars, cause your house is too full of family to get any privacy?"

"I never did this before."

"Serious?"

"Yep. Despite my acknowledged sex god status, I barely dated in high school. And then I met Sus the first day of college, and never dated anyone else until after we divorced."

She sat up a little. "Does it bug you, talking about her?"

My heart lurched a little at this evidence Margo wanted to know me more deeply. I reminded myself she was leaving. "No. I mean, I can't with my family. They treat me like a cipher, and Susanne was their way into understanding me. So for years after we divorced, they kept inviting her around or asking about her or staring at me like they had no idea how to coax words out of me."

"Ouch."

I shrugged. "Not saying I'm not part of that pattern, but, yeah. It ...was no fun. It's not like that so much now, but it doesn't help that they all think I'm deeply religious."

Now she sat fully away from me. "Wait. You're not?"

I grabbed her hand and set it back on my erection. "That's a surprise to you?"

When I released her, she kept palming me for a delicious moment. Then she straddled me, but sat back instead of indulging in that youthful dry-humping she'd been talking about. "The whole church music director thing seemed like a clue to the importance of your faith."

"It's the music. I love the music. Which all started in church for me, as a kid, but ... I'm not exactly secular, I'm not saying that. And not saying that deeply religious people can't be super horny; that was—okay, I was going to call it a joke, but it was deflection." This was harder to articulate than the feelings behind my divorce. I looked at the night sky past Margo's shoulders, like a shooting star might appear to deliver the right words to me. "I guess it's that my faith isn't tied to religion. I do find it, find God, in the music, more than anywhere else. And in helping voices come together to rise up in celebration. But also, it's everywhere. In Parsley running at the waves, and in this gorgeous sky. In tacos, as long as no one sneaks spinach into them. In kissing you."

"It's part of your foundation."

"Yes." I breathed the word more than said it; she'd

found a simple way to express something so profound about me.

The kiss we shared then sank deep, as if I was sealing a new way to define myself into my heart. But when I pulled back, I caught a flash of sorrow on her face. "Do you want to talk about it?"

She shook her head without asking what I meant, but nestled into my side and gradually relaxed as I held her. After a moment, she said, "I keep telling myself it's not fair to be mad at him. He's got this awesome chance to do the work he wants, and God knows he deserves to live in the community he's already found up there."

"But?"

She huffed a laugh. "But. Exactly. It's not even that I feel like I've been a placeholder in his life. The person he bosses around and laughs with because we barely left our apartment for so long. That's not even right, not really, because you should see the guy's online communities; he's always on some discussion board or another."

We listened to the waves. I stroked her arm. "He's your best friend."

Her head dropped hard against my shoulder. "He's my best friend. I'm his. We've known we were going to stop living together sooner or later; we've both been searching. But to be so far apart? And he didn't once tell me about it? I shouldn't be angry."

"You can be, though."

She groaned. "Can I? It's not too petulant and left-out baby sister of me? It's not a sign of how much I've depended on Cole being in my life, that I can't even let him take this step without pouting that he never mentioned it to me first?"

"Margo. It's okay to be mad, it's fine that you're sad

about his moving. You can understand why he's done it this way and be excited for him and still have your own reactions. Best friend doesn't mean a hundred percent good feelings, any more than being siblings does."

"I know."

"Of course you do."

She leaned in to kiss my cheek. "Thanks. I needed to vent it out. And probably, I need to admit that I've had this idea of traveling and working while I see the country and experience new things, and that's what thrills me, but all along? I had this idea of Cole, and our apartment, as some kind of safety net. An in-case place to go if I need it."

Damn my foolhardy urge to offer up my bed as an alternative. I swallowed that back and said, "You don't need it, I don't think. You're bright and adaptable and talented and confident. I have faith you're going to fly high. And you'll be able to tell Cole about all of it—he'll want to hear about all of it—no matter where you each live."

Margo ran her hands up my shoulders and drew me in for a long kiss. And instead of suggesting she could also tell me about all of her adventures, I drew a blanket higher around us and set about making up for all my lost chances to make out in cars, in the past, and, I feared, in our future.

CHAPTER
FIFTEEN
MARGO

Most nights that week, we slept at Karl's. He came to mine on Tuesday, since I had an early shift on the front desk the next morning, but it was easier, with Parsley, for me to be on his turf. Not to mention, even the decent bathroom and sizable kitchenette in my single room at the hotel did little to make it feel like anything but a place to mark time before I left.

Wednesday night, he was leading a choir rehearsal, and I showed up at my family home for dinner. Mama handed me an apron even as she kissed me, which served me right for mentioning how hard it was to cook at the hotel. I'd only blurted that out as an excuse to stop her from dragging me to the markets with her, when I'd made plans with Karl. But it meant she'd decided we should prep a few dinners I could reheat in my kitchenette.

The obvious solution was telling her we'd been cooking in Karl's decently appointed kitchen and I didn't need to haul around a bunch of prepped meals. Except that would trigger round ninety-four or so of the 'why not just move back home for good' conversation.

So I assembled enchiladas for dinner and for later, then chopped piles of tomatoes to get a start on the salsas for our tamalada. I felt an unpleasant twinge at the reminder of how close Christmas was, and how that meant I needed to line up my next job. My next destination.

"Cole told you about his move?" I asked when Dad came in.

Dad hugged my shoulders and kissed the top of my head. "You'll be okay, Gogo."

I narrowed my eyes. "I know I'll be okay."

"We're just reminding you. We know you'll miss him," Mama said.

"But even when he's far away, he's still your big brother. And you've got us. Did I tell you the other day I cleared all those old toys we'd been saving out of your bedroom closet? Boxed up a bunch of the board games from your bookshelf, too."

"You got rid of my knock-off Barbie Dream House?"

Dad scoffed. "Of all my kids, you were always the least interested in playing dolls. Anyway, Larissa told me which things were worth preserving for grandkids, and to find new homes for the rest. And this way, there's lots more room for you."

"Dad."

"Not saying you have to move home. But it never hurts to have the option, especially if you're clearing out of Austin."

And that was the crux. No matter how much I said I wasn't interested in settling down in Rockport, Mama and Dad kept talking like I didn't know my own mind.

I knew my damn mind.

What I didn't know was how to make them see that.

"You're almost twenty-five," Mama said. "It's time to get serious about your future."

"Maybe that's true," I said. "But my future is not here. It's out there. I want to travel and work different places and figure some things out along the way. In the present. That's what I'm focused on."

"Your sisters ..."

"I'm not them. Can't you let me be me?"

Mama sighed and shook her head, but Dad patted my shoulder and went to set the table.

When I left, I was restless. I drove around for a while, but a town the size of Rockport, there weren't a whole lot of distractions around every corner. Especially not distractions grand enough to keep me from ruminating over what was around the corner for my life. Cole had talked about pro-con lists, but I'd never been one for that kind of determined decision-making. I didn't have goals to work towards via a series of broken-down chunks, or spreadsheets with five-year plans.

What I had was gut feelings. I had things that fascinated me, and the desire to investigate them for as long as they stayed important to me. I had the ability to do any number of jobs to keep myself funded while I explored. I had core interests: going to concerts, being on the sea, getting way too involved in taking care of the people I loved.

That last one was the problem I needed to solve. I loved Cole; I loved everyone in my family. But I'd thrown myself into Project: Protect My Big Brother when I was a teenager. He'd tucked me under his wing when I needed him, and I'd tried to hold an umbrella over us in return. Even though we'd both been walking steady on our own for ages now, it still shook me up when he cut me off from my self-appointed gig. Not because he needed protection—not more than any of the other humans being unjustly vilified and targeted just for living as themselves—but because I had to face how I'd let those protective tendencies become a key to my personality. How could I embrace living my own life if I kept looking back to be sure he was okay living his?

What sucked about the abrupt way he'd told me about his move was that I kept saying I was sailing out into uncharted waters on my own, and his news made me realize that all along, I'd been clinging to Cole as a safety line.

I had to cut that line, and navigate to the next cove entirely on my own. It was thrilling, but also terrifying.

Ruminating about journeys, I ended up at the marina. I loved the peaceful ocean smell, the gentle clang of rigging and shush of waves crashing against the pilings. I sat on a dock and stared out at the dark water, letting my mind wander. The breeze cut sideways, whipping my hair around me until I turned to face the wind. I caught sight of a spire in the distance.

It wasn't St. Luke's, but it lodged in my breastbone just the same. Talking with Karl about his faith the other day had stirred up feelings I'd been setting aside, and now they rushed at me like an incoming tide.

I'd been mad when Cole tossed the accusation at me, but one thing he was right about was that I'd been a very religious teenager. Youth group, Sunday school aide, teen night lock-ins, choirs, the works. St. Patrick's had made up a lot of my world, and I'd gone there assuming that my love for God meant there was no question of the Church's support of me. I'd been to confession after the abortion, and not even mentioned it, because God's love meant it wasn't wrong for me to exercise my choice over my decision. And then Father James spewed his intolerance and bigotry, and that was it. I walked away from my faith and refused to look back.

Until now.

It was easy enough to attend the handbell rehearsals and perform at services while telling myself it was because I enjoyed the instrument. And really, really enjoyed the conductor, as a side benefit.

It was harder to admit that being in St. Luke's itself had been an unexpected balm. And to concede the importance of looking at faith in different ways than the one I'd known growing up. To look for God in music and on the waves and in my love for my siblings. To accept that if I made the choice to trust in that love, it would buoy me up no matter how the tides of our lives changed. That choice was a form of faith, and until Cole made me walk back in to a physical church, I'd been rejecting any kind of belief that reminded me too much of being a broken-hearted seventeen year old.

I wasn't that girl now. I wasn't moved to add any kind of organized religion back to my life, but I was coming to understand that it did my grown-ass soul a lot of good to let in new forms of faith.

I sighed. The single-serving meals in my passenger seat needed refrigeration. It didn't surprise me at all when I ended up carrying them, and my overnight bag, straight to Karl's door.

CHAPTER
SIXTEEN
KARL

We rehearsed *Joy to the World* as part of the Gaudete Sunday repertoire. I was reviewing the martelatto technique for everyone ("Remember, don't lift the bell more than five inches above the pad, it'll damage them. Keep it horizontal and ring straight down.") Margo kept twitching her nose at me, and somehow her mirth spread to Parsley. Normally my dog kept herself snug on her mat in the corner during rehearsals, but she wandered over and belly crawled under the bell tables until she could plant her head on Margo's feet.

I gave her a questioning look, and she just smiled at me. It set all those embers of anticipation crackling through my chest, as if we hadn't been reveling in each other every night.

I clapped my hands to get rehearsal—and myself—back on schedule. Ignoring all my anticipation of getting her alone.

As we walked to my house after, Margo tucked her arm into mine and pressed close as if to ward off the tinge of cold in the air. Parsley danced beside us, full of her own pleasure about us all strolling in the winter weather together.

"Oh, hey, I made up my own Parsley song," Margo said. "Wanna hear?"

My own tail would be wagging, if I had one. "Of course."

She cleared her throat, filled her diaphragm, and launched in. "Hark how the dog / Sweet silky dog / Wants me to say / I'll toss balls her way / Fetch time is here / Bring that ball here / Dogs young and old / Seek balls of gold / Sweet-dog, Sweet-dog."

"Merry, merry, merry, fetch time," I sang, and she joined me on the refrain.

Her mezzo-soprano and my tenor harmonized into something light and bright and bold. Her take on *Carol of the Bells* amused me. But the intent pounding of my heart came from a broader place than these few minutes together.

I'd lived alone for a few years before adopting Parsley, and as soon as she was in my life, I started singing to her. Sure, I'd sung plenty before then: joining in with something I was streaming; testing out a few bars while skimming for music to bring to a choir; belting Beyonce in the shower. But Parsley immediately became the inspiration and audience and co-host of the Karl and Parsley show.

So I had a huge repertoire of Parsley-themed songs. I didn't exactly hide them from others—my friends, people who slept over, anyone who passed us on our walks. It wasn't any kind of secret shame.

But no one had ever participated in this dog tunes thing with me. No one had offered us a song of their own.

I squeezed her to me and kissed her cheek. "I love it."

January.

She was leaving in January.

Over reheated enchiladas, a comment about Margo's mom reminded me to warn her. "Head's up. I guess my family decided to attend Sunday's service. They'll be asking you to join us for lunch after."

She set down her fork. "They will?"

I didn't love how still she'd gone. I nodded. "My parents, a sister. Maybe my brother, too, but I'm not sure."

"And they want to meet me?"

"Yeah, so it seems my brother is dating Matt the Grace's niece. And you know what a gossip Matt the Grace is. So is my brother, turns out, because my whole family knows we're seeing each other. The girlfriend apparently talked like it was obvious they'd drive up for one of my services, like she was doing for Matt and Paul. So now a whole lot of them are showing up. And they'll ask you to lunch."

Now she was even more upright and unfocused. It was like she was putting all her energy into navigating unseen currents so she wouldn't be swept away. I couldn't find the right lifeline to throw her. "It's just—they're curious about you. They won't make it something big. More than anything, it's what I told you before, about them not under-standing me. So anything that gives them something new to talk to me about, they latch on."

The look she sent me. It put me in mind of the wild horses that gave Mustang Island its name. Of course, unlike many of the barrier islands just north of it, Mustang had long since been paved and cultivated with resorts and vaca-tion homes and golf courses. All that lost wildness and tamed wilderness. It sapped my joy to think of how the island could never recapture that freedom.

I cleared my throat, then stood to clear the table. "It's

not a problem if you don't want to go. They'll find other ways to talk to me. I am their son; they've known me for decades. It shouldn't be all that difficult."

Margo stacked my dishwasher in silence, giving me plenty of time to replay my statement. To debate. If I came up with more words, might I sound less bitter, or less stuck in the rut my family grooved out for me long ago? Or would I just scrape more mud against the moorings?

A passing motorcycle caused Parsley to woof, which I took as an excuse to give her a quick walk. Some nights, Margo accompanied us on this last stroll around the block, but she made no move to join us. I forced myself to sing to my dog as we went, but as quick as she trotted back to the house once her business was done, I don't think she was charmed.

Margo was sitting with a cup of tea when we returned. She patted the sofa, which meant Parsley leapt to snuggle her. "That's not who I meant, you big goof."

I relaxed a fraction at her affectionate tone, and sat on the other side of the dog, who was delighted to offer both her belly and her muzzle for our attention. "So," I said.

"So," she agreed.

"It's not a big deal that we're together, right? That my family knows?" I kept my voice low. "I mean, Margo, you have to know I value what we have. Even though it's new, even though it's never going to have a chance to get old. Even though you're in no way responsible for my feelings about it. About you. It's—the thing is, you're opening up some ways of thinking for me, and that matters. You matter."

"I'm not staying."

"I didn't ask you to stay." My reply was too quick. Too revealing of how much I hated saying the words. I paced myself and continued. "I wouldn't ask. Nothing's changed for you. Nothing's changed for me, come to that. I still plan on a life right here. I want to live in Rockport. I want to repaint my study. I want the Church Council to approve my request for new music folders. I want a partner. I want to be a dad. I get how all that puts me on the wrong side of a chasm from you. I get that no matter how dynamic you and I are, you're young, and you have all these other pursuits to, um, pursue. So that leaves us with a chasm, and I can't fly over it, or ask you to fly over it to me, or ... this is getting away from me. But I know, at the heart of the matter, that nothing's changed."

She scrubbed Parsley's ears and didn't look at me. Quietly repeated, "Nothing's changed."

And no matter what impractical fantasies I might dream up, she was only agreeing to the truth.

CHAPTER
SEVENTEEN

MARGO

The lobby Christmas decorations nearly blew a fuse, and a large group's tour of the wildlife refuge needed quick scramble fixes thanks to a minibus breakdown, and also, I couldn't find the pink sweater I'd planned to wear to church.

I went anyway. I definitely didn't think about taking a kayak and launching off that nice calm beach behind the regional airport where Karl and I had stargazed. Or about calling Cole to demand we buddy rewatch a few episodes of *Our Flag Means Death*. Or about zipping down to Corpus to take Aunt Maxima to brunch.

Nope.

I put on my blue sweater, and arrived at the parish hall in plenty of time to grab my chorister's robes and bell ringer's gloves and one of the roses Karl had gathered for everyone to wear. I stuck it in my hair, clipped over my orange streak. I smiled at him as I took my place for the processional. His return look tried to pin me in place, which was foolish of him because Matt the Grace was already leading the low bells towards the sanctuary.

Karl's pursed lips made him a touch stern and I nearly broke into a bit of a swoon. Instead, I glanced down to check my bells were oriented correctly and slid into place between the other Graces. After that, we were just musician and conductor. I didn't seek messages in his posture or expression between pieces. He didn't deviate from any of the work of the service, moving between the handbells and the vocalists and the piano with his usual sharp, observant skill. He was always where he needed to be, not rushing, and it struck me how deliberate that was. He built the music part of worship in a way that he carried all the moving parts with him. And balanced them effectively with the content of the service, so it all built into something robust and satisfying.

And, given that we were on the third Sunday of Advent, full of joy.

Instead of studying him any more than necessary, I looked out to the congregation. This close to Christmas, the pews teemed with faces. Most, of course, I didn't know. I wasn't trying to pick out Karl's family, though one guy over on the left looked a hell of a lot like my memory of Karl when I first knew him.

Funny how he was such a different person now. More filled out. More solid. Like he possessed a special amount of gravitational pull. It wasn't just that his jaw was squarer, or his crow's feet, or arms that definitely had been scrawnier back in his early twenties. Karl possessed a self-confidence that didn't blare to the rafters, but shone there anyway. And an edge to his posture, a determination. I saw it sometimes in the way he could make me laugh, but sometimes just in the way he could look at me and make the world feel crowded with possibilities.

With dreams.

Dreams that were vital to him.

I glanced over at my parents, and was grinning before I fully grasped that they were sitting next to my sister Emmeline. She was our baby, the last Dunway still in college, and I'd thought she'd be on campus until later in the week. Her head was down—likely reading her phone in her lap—but as Karl moved to us to signal *Joy to the World*, Dad nudged her shoulder and she looked up. I got a mouthed 'hi' from her as she removed her earbuds to pay attention to our music.

After that, I had to start watching Karl's hands again. They commanded us all, deftly ensuring the peal rang twice through before adding the choir voices, then inviting the whole congregation to sing out.

I wasn't surprised that it was all more than Emmeline, with her auditory processing disorder, wanted to encounter. While the music resounded, and most everyone in St. Luke's swayed and smiled, she slipped out.

When it was all over, and I'd collected my jacket and purse, I found her just where I'd suspected: tucked in the little gazebo between the courtyard and the parish house. "Emmers!"

She squeezed me tight. "Gogo!"

"Why didn't you text me you'd be here? I thought you had finals still?"

"All I've got left are two essays, and I decided I'd rather work on them from home." She hooked our arms together. "So, surprise, I'm back until January. Now you don't have to be the only child the elders rope into hanging Christmas lights."

I kissed her cheek. "Bless you. You should hear Uncle Bill's plans for the holiday party. He thinks Mama and Dad should hire a party tent and a dance floor. Like, with a stage and everything. Not for the yard—he wants to block off the street and invite the neighbors."

"But we're still the ones cooking all the food?"

"Logistics were never his strength. I pointed that out, and he said Jeannie could probably figure it all out for us."

Emmeline snorted. Our second sister ate logistics for breakfast, lunch, and midnight snack. Or maybe it was her rocker husband's apple pie at midnight, but only cause she'd already eaten all the logistics. Only problem was, Jeannie and Brendan were on tour and not due to Rockport until the day before the annual Dunway December party. "I'm so glad I get to be the one to share this scheme in the sibling chat."

"Oh, that's not all," I told her. "Go talk to Bill and Sam. They decided we should add glitter to the equation."

"What now?"

"They want an ornament-decorating table. In the house." I was ready to give her the convoluted rundown of how they'd proposed the idea, but Karl came up behind Emmeline, his eyes burning with some feeling sharper than the sternness from before services.

"Margo."

I reached to rest my hand on his forearm. "Karl, this is Emmeline. She's back for Christmas break early. Emmers, it's Karl Moore."

My sister's gaze tracked all the nonverbal cues of the situation and came to rest on me with an expression that told me she'd rescue me if I needed it. She was polite with Karl, who for his part put on his 'I work here' mask. But he took my hand and cradled it in his own like a gift. As always, the heat of his palm radiated into me, and I read in it a message of banked impatience. But tolerance, too.

Emmeline slipped away to, she said, talk down Sam and Uncle Bill, leaving me and Karl alone.

"I thought—are you coming to meet my family?"

"I didn't know Em would be here this week. I wanted to find out what's up, and I told you before it's not easy for her to have conversations in crowds."

He nodded, but he was still wearing the choir director mask. "Will you come now? Or is that not going to happen?"

I glanced at the group blatantly observing us, which included his young look-alike, in case I was unsure of their identity. I tugged at the cuff of my blue sweater, suddenly determined to see for myself if this judgmental handful of Karl's relatives failed to value him. "Of course."

The look he gave me then broke through any reserve he might have been trying to maintain.

I wasn't going to tuck myself in to his life in the long term, but before I left, I could damn sure point out to the Moore family the many facets of Karl worth their notice.

CHAPTER

EIGHTEEN

KARL

The family took me and Margo to get dim sum. She didn't demur when they invited her, and I didn't delude myself that she accepted with her whole heart. As expected, they bombarded her with questions. Nothing more than anodyne comments about the service for me, but for her, they were curious and opinionated.

Margo was polite, but I could tell she was uncomfortable. I was uncomfortable too. This was something they always did: directed all of their conversation through whoever I brought along. I should be used to it, but I kept trying to initiate conversations only to watch my olive branches die on the trunk. I used to think it was sweet that they put effort into making my dates comfortable. I used to hope those efforts could be a bridge to them knowing me, not as the self-isolating oldest kid who got grumpy at how many baseball games everyone else in the family was playing in, but as an adult. Someone to find common ground with.

Instead, they'd get cozy with my date and continue not talking to me.

101

And now they played out the same pattern with Margo, even though I'd been clear with them that she wasn't staying in Rockport. Even though they knew that by the time of Dad's February birthday dinner, I'd be showing up alone again.

Instead of responding to Margo's compliment of Mom's flower earrings—she didn't even glance my way to show she remembered they were a gift from me—Mom asked, "And Karl taught you how to ring the handbells?"

"Back when I was in high school, yeah. I hadn't picked them up since I was seventeen, but he's a great director. Getting back into the swing of things was easy."

My brother Aiden laughed. "That's a bell pun, right?"

I took more spare ribs. Offered the steamed pork bun basket to Margo. Her hand lingered on mine when she took it, which meant a ridiculous amount. She turned back to Aiden. "I think we've heard every ringers pun in the English language out of your brother."

No one took the bait. Even my dad had moved right past the opportunity to engage in a pun war.

The next time I noticed her trying to hype me, Margo was deflecting Mom's nosiness about what she would do next by saying, "I know people who have always know what they were passionate about. I don't even mean paid work—I think it's great to have a generic job and make time for your passions outside of that. Most people live that way, after all. But, like with my sister Jeannie; she worked for the Chamber of Commerce because she loves her town, and organizing, and making her community a great place for everyone. Her passion for those things helped her to get the kind of paid work that meant she could do them, even if she also had less-fun tasks to do. Or like Karl, how he deals with the Church Council and admin stuff and sometimes being the only one around to move the tables, but most of his time, he gets to work with the music he loves. Choosing the right pieces to enhance the liturgy, guiding people of varied abilities into harmony together, teaching and empowering them to express themselves through music. It's amazing to see, and mostly that's because he's bringing all of himself to the work he does. I don't know what my version of that is yet, but that's what I crave."

Even with Aiden rolling his eyes and Dad glancing away to look for more sticky rice, I had to drop a kiss on Margo's cheek. She'd talked about this before, but—call me egocentric—it clicked for me, hearing her map the journeys she desired on what she said while defending me.

Not that the defense would change anything. I'd get awkward questions about Margo the first few times I saw my family in the new year, and then they'd stop asking, and then I'd be the quiet one in the corner again.

Still. It was nice she tried.

Margo and I went back to my place after lunch. After walking Parsley, who indicated she'd suffered mightily by being left at home for the entirety of a Sunday service and lunch afterwards, we tried to watch a movie. I gave up on it pretty quick, cause it was too hard to keep my hands off of her.

I wanted to worship every curve and dip of her body, awed that she saw me so clearly. And that she seemed impressed with who I was, with no expectation I'd learn to talk sports, or stop filling my weekends with church stuff, or aim for a higher-paid career that meant making music was relegated to the margins of my life.

The parts of me she championed to my family so deeply aligned with who I strived to be. She didn't ask me to be apologetic or guilty about my family's failed expectations. "I'm going to eat you out right now."

"Is that some kind of threat?" She widened her legs, which made it tougher to whisk down her pants. But it gave me room to wedge between them as I knelt on the floor.

"I kind of consider it more of a sacred duty. I know you never wanted all that. You were kinder then you needed to be."

She cupped my cheek, and it felt like tenderness. Like something more. "Being kind wasn't a chore, Karl. They're nice people, and they were mostly nice to me. Plus the dim sum was delicious."

"It was. It even made up for Aiden. Mostly."

Laughing, Margo lifted her hips so I could wrangle off her pants and underwear. "He wasn't bad. He gave me the last soup dumpling."

I kissed her from knee to hip, very much done discussing my brother. Or anyone in my family. She opened her legs to me, giving me an unobstructed view of her glistening pussy. I leaned in, ravenous, and licked from her clit to her opening. She gasped, arching her back, and I repeated the movement, this time dipping my tongue inside her. I moaned into her sweetness as I continued to lick and tease her. Her breathing was coming in short gasps now, and her hands fisted the couch cushions as she writhed beneath me.

The sharp scent of her arousal, the way she drummed her ankle at my back, the memory of her implacable defense of me at lunch. I was hard as the bronze of the bells, and as likely to fracture if I didn't get into her soon. But she was close. So close. Her clit pulsed, and I wanted her to come so hard. I kept teasing her until she was panting and moaning and bucking her hips at my face. Finally, I succumbed to her demands and pressed my tongue firmly against her clit as I simultaneously sent two in pursuit of her G-spot. She came instantly, crying out and clawing at me as she rode the waves of pleasure.

When I kissed my way up her belly, shoving her shirt up as I went, her hands went to my head, stroking me absently the way she did after orgasm.

Languid. She was languid, and my chest expanded with each brush of her fingertips through my hair. I peeled off her shirt and bra, then my own shirt.

When I stood, her hands fell to her chest, and she began to brush those fingertips over her hardening nipples. Her eyes were closed, but she smiled—still so languid—when I unzipped my pants. She licked her lips and plucked slowly at her nipples and I didn't bother with kicking off the rest of my clothes. I just yanked out my cock and fisted it hard as I watched her slide around until she lay with her legs hanging over the sofa's arm.

At last she opened her eyes, and she was looking straight at my pumping hand. "You gonna feed that to me?"

Christ. This woman. I managed to strip the rest of the way as she watched, humming quietly, then I braced one knee by her hip, and one hand on the back cushion, and leaned in.

Margo swirled her tongue around my cock, teasing before taking it into her mouth. At first she was as gentle as she'd been with her breasts, but soon was sucking at me in earnest. I wasn't quite thrusting, but her hand on my balls guided me to lean deeper, and she took more of me in.

I kept saying her name, over and over, a litany of, "Margo, God, Margo. Margo." She watched me with those deep brown eyes full of desire and lust. And then my balls were tight, and my spine was tense, and my hips were demanding more. I brushed back her hair, and she hummed, and I nearly whimpered. Below me, she wriggled against the couch, like she needed the friction as badly as I needed the motion.

I pulled away and scrambled for a condom. And as soon as I was fully seated in her, I knew, to my complete doom, that I'd fallen in love.

NINETEEN

MARGO

I woke with a hook lodged in my chest. I made a massive effort to extract myself from Karl's bed without flailing or scrambling or leaving a cartoon shape of my body fleeing through his walls.

It wasn't cold. No chill in the air seeping into his place. I wouldn't go diving into the Gulf in a bikini or anything, but there was no atmospheric reason for me to shiver as I scooped up my clothes and ducked into the bathroom.

I had to sneak out. If Karl woke up and saw me, he would start to talk about emotions. I'd seen the look in his eye when we were fucking. Heard the tenderness in his voice when he lured me from his couch to his bed. Felt the possession in his hold when we curled together to sleep. So I made a silent getaway.

Or, I tried to. But while I was dressing by the faint glow of the medicine cabinet light, Parsley left her dog bed and took over the warm spot I'd left behind. Her thumping tail smacked Karl's bare abdomen, and he woke to see me across the room.

"Margo," he said, groggy voice cracking a little.

"Early shift," I tried. Lied.

He sighed. "Running away from your feelings won't solve anything."

I watched as he sat up, my heart jumping like it could make the escape I hadn't managed. What light shot through the curtain gap showed me all his rumpled, sheets-tangled, singular appeal. His legs stirring under the covers like they missed tangling with mine. His abdomen, tense with the strength he'd so often used when bringing me pleasure. His broad shoulders, ready to bear any burdens if only I would let him.

If only I'd gotten out sooner. "I'm not trying to solve anything. There's nothing to solve."

Parsley rolled over to press herself into Karl's side, like I needed a reminder that on top of the rest of his appeal, he came with the best dog in Texas. She gave a sigh that Karl echoed. "If that's true, what's with the running?"

I tugged on my sweater. "It's not running. I'm sticking with my plan."

"Right. Your plan." His scoff told me all I needed to hear about what he really thought of me.

If that was how he felt, why was I holding back my own opinions?

I shook my head. "Do you know that when you talk about your divorce, you bring up how y'all were too young to know your own minds? How you didn't give yourselves the chance to figure out what was most important to you each, and what it meant when those things weren't the same? And every time, you're looking at me like, 'hey, Margo, how about you tell me exactly what's important to you?' Like you haven't know from day one that what matters to me is the exploration itself. It's great you know what matters to you, Karl. But however rough your path to get there, you've had the time to figure it out. I'm not you—not you now, and not you, or Susanne for that matter, back when you were my age. I'm me, and I deserve to know what that means when I'm not conforming to anyone else's expectations. Not my family's, not society's, not yours."

I backed to the door, that hook in my chest insistent about me leaving before he could hear any tears in my voice. "I don't know if your desire for a partner and kids and this job in this town means you think you can just sit back and slot whoever you're dating like a puzzle piece into your life. But, Karl, I'm not a puzzle piece. You can't take my not being definite about my future as free rein to force me into the shape you need."

Karl came to stand in front of me. "I ... that's what you think I'm doing? That's how I make you feel? I know you're not interchangeable, Margo. It's—that's so far from what you are, to me. If I showed you any kind of unfinished puzzle, it wasn't to force you into anything. Not deliberately. It was only to show how I have space for you, if you decided to stay here while you figure out the next thing. I don't want to change anything except you applying an arbitrary deadline to the end of us. If you spend a few more weeks in Rockport while you sort out what's next? A few more weeks with me? Wouldn't we both enjoy that?" His voice was as stripped down to nakedness as his body, and all of his conductor's intensity was focused solidly on me.

I swallowed hard and looked away. It would have been easier to fight my need to respond if he'd matched my frantic anger with heat of his own, instead of breaking me with his raw warmth. "You knew all this when we began," I said. "You always knew I was leaving."

"I know I did. I'm not saying you weren't always honest. I'd never say that, Margo. Your honesty and your bravery and your confidence, those are some of your treasures. But I guess, somewhere along the way—I guess I started hoping you'd imagine something different. Hoping what I feel for you isn't one-sided. Hoping you'd want to add it to the treasures of your life."

My breath shuddered out. I wasn't falling for some kind of trap built up entirely of his compliments and his emotions and his delayed dreams. "You're hoping I'll stay because you're lonely and I make you feel good."

He caught my hand before I could turn away. Tugged me close. "It's not only about feeling good, Margo. It can be about more than that. We can be about so much more, if—"

"No." I made to yank free, but he held on tighter. "Karl, it's not enough. I know Rockport; I know myself in Rockport. My whole life here, I searched and only found things that were wrong for me. I don't mean only because of St. Pat's, but you saw for yourself how that gossip is still a nest of rattlers coming out of hibernation. I'm not going to start fitting in, and finding myself, if I'm stuck here. It's been great, these nights with you, but you're building castles in the air and I need to stay firmly on the ground."

"Margo—"

"No," I said again, softer this time. "I can't do this. You need to let me go. Let me leave."

His grip on my hand loosened and then fell away entirely, like mooring line gone slack. I turned and left without looking back.

CHAPTER

TWENTY

KARL

Every person who'd been at that lunch texted me over the next couple of days to rave about Margo. Every person but Margo.

With every message, her words about empty castles and broken puzzles tumbled through me. Her vital need to make independent strides. Her confident rejection of the elements I'd built into my life. Her painful refusal to hear how I felt about her. Her heartbreaking decision that I wasn't worth her time.

I texted back to Mom and Dad that she'd enjoyed meeting them, too. To my brother that it wasn't a serious relationship. To my sister—the only one to mention our Gaudete service—that I'd be happy to teach her to play handbells, too.

I took Parsley to a secluded stretch of beach, trying to clear my head. The tide was in, waves creeping high along the shore. Gulls soared overhead, screeching. Parsley ran ahead of me, sniffing at seaweed and straining in her eagerness to get me to run up the dunes with her. I'd left behind my earbuds, so I knew there weren't any reckless ATVs

111

cresting the sand this time, but I balked at the idea of indulging in that game anymore. Dr. Meyers had given her the all-clear. It was only my fear that kept Parsley reined in.

She wasn't happy with my display of cowardice. Or maybe it was that I'd barely sung a word to her all week. Or maybe I wasn't the only one who missed Margo.

Was my fear reining me in, too? Keeping me tied to my plans for the future, tied to this golden vision I had of making my life right here, walking these beaches, attending St. Luke's, making music and making a family with someone stunningly like Margo?

No. My dreams grew out of years of my life. Years of therapy during my marriage as we tried to reconcile our desires, and after, as I reframed my life on my own. Years of coming to terms with the distance from my parents, and with my urge to be a dad, to build my own family with careful hands. My counselor had helped me see how I conceived of this hypothetical family as a do-over of my own disconnected and isolated childhood. Until now, I hadn't thought of these goals as harmful to me.

As Parsley and I stared out at the water, I examined the part myself that had pigeonholed Margo. In so many ways, she was perfect—we shared values and interests, we fit together temperamentally and physically. She could so easily be the true partner I'd dreamed of. The family I craved.

If not for all the ways we didn't fit.

It ached, how much I was in love with Margo. Not just infatuated with or lusting after her, but treacherously, deliriously in love with her.

And what were her dreams? We'd talked about her desire to travel, to try other jobs, to explore. She'd claimed Rockport couldn't give her any of that. Maybe it was feeling out of step with her devout family, maybe it was the ways a small town can lock you into a version of yourself that's based on the views of those around you. Her visions of city life. Whatever her reasons, it wasn't my place to question them.

What I needed to know, though, was: could part of her journey include, someday, making a life with me?

I'd spend every hour since she walked away coming up with counter-arguments and pleas and gestures of faith I could make to show her that I didn't intend to mold her into some preordained shape.

I didn't. She was bright and free and beautiful and fierce just as she was.

I longed for her, just as she was.

But I also hadn't reshaped any of my dreams to fit around her.

I patted my thigh to get Parsley moving back towards my truck. The emptiness of my life would have to wait until after rehearsal. Until she wasn't standing in my workplace, taking my direction, but unwilling to take my love.

She was there, at least. Avoiding me by letting the Graces circle her for a detailed rehash of the previous Sunday's performance. The Grace who was on the Church Council gave me one of her significant looks and mimed scrolling on a cellphone, so I stepped to the back doorway while the last of the ringers filed in.

Sure enough, there was an email setting up a meeting for the next Monday. Maybe I'd get the new music folders after all? But too many of my guesses lately left me crumbled in dust, so I didn't know how much hope I should be mustering.

I didn't know how much hope I ever would be able to muster.

I mounted my podium and called everyone to order, gladder than I'd ever been for my rehearsal schedules. Margo did everything with her usual confident grace, not missing a note, not flubbing a technique. Giving me no reason to speak directly to her. No reason to stare at the flash of pink that now nestled next to the orange streak in her hair. No reason to wonder if her hands trembled, even a little bit, within her bell ringer's gloves.

No reason for any of that floating hope I couldn't decide about.

TWENTY-ONE

MARGO

I escaped rehearsal, zigzagging through the room to avoid Karl and his soulful eyes. At least he'd left Parsley behind, so I didn't have to evade her affection on my way out, too.

I swung by home for Emmeline, and we went for drinks. Tucked into the back booth of a quiet bar, Christmas lights twinkling around us but fortunately no carols playing to plague either of us, I told her about hooking up with Karl since Thanksgiving. And about our fight.

"So, now it's over," I said. Declared. Affirmed, like there was no chance I was wrong.

"Hmm." Emmeline sipped her strawberry margarita. "Okay. And to be clear, if you weren't in quest mode right now, he wouldn't be the right kind of partner for you?"

Her question reminded me of how I once imagined Karl —Mr. Moore—as my ideal. But that was the fantasy of a kid spinning tales out of sweet sounds and silliness.

And now?

I couldn't quite manage shaking my head, but I made a grumpy negative sound. Because no matter how much I liked about the Karl I now knew—his intense charm, and his competence, and the way he gathered up diverse people and created harmony, and how he was a perfect fuck—I couldn't get into a cycle of thinking he was the only guy in the world for me. The only one who could amuse me over dinner, and wow me in bed, and listen for the truth underlying my tales, and expand my worldview, and make up silly dog songs, and buy boxes of tea in case I came around, and find the perfect fit for our hands to hold each other when we walked.

I sighed. "There's no point wondering what shifting around nine hundred moving parts of the space-time continuum might mean. Those parts haven't moved, and they're not going to. I'm the one in the wind."

My sister stared me down. "I was fifteen when you went to college."

I bit my lips together, not sure where she was going with this.

"Larissa was already married. Jeannie was off in Jackrabbit. Sarita had just gotten out of college and settled in Austin. Home was just you and me and sometimes Cole, and then Cole left, and right after, so did you."

"Shit, Emmers. Was that rough?"

She laughed and slurped up the dregs of her drink. "It was blissful. It was so quiet, and no one was put out by being forced to drive me to therapy or the ortho, and if I asked for Greek food we could have Greek food with no complaints that it was supposed to be lasagna night."

"Last year I made pastitsio on lasagna night and Cole nearly moved out. I sent him like five links of places calling it Greek lasagna, but he said I was determined to deprive him of life's only reliable pleasure."

Emmeline pointed at me. "Exactly. I had three beautiful

years of none of that. The elders were benignly indulgent, no one tossed opinions at me. It was the best."

I looked into my own glass, debating a third Negroni. They were watered down, and I was still in a bummed out mode, but I did have to face hotel customers in the morning. "So, I'm glad you enjoyed all that and I'm sorry I never asked about it before, but why are you telling me now?"

"Gogo, it wasn't just the freedom to put my faves in the dinner rotation. It was the time to think about my life. To discover mind-blowing shit in my physics class, when I never knew before that I even liked science. And that was cause no one in the family liked science. Why would I figure, if all five of my older siblings shuddered at Mr. Burkholder's name, that it would turn out his class was the best thing I'd ever taken?"

"I still can't believe how, of all your awards, the certificate for being Burkholder's top student is the one thing you hung above your desk."

"Can't you? Sure, he can really drone on, but that certificate matters to me, the way the swim trophies or whatever don't. It reminds me where I was when I knew what I loved. Maybe I'd still have gotten to know that about myself if half my siblings still lived at home, taking up physical and mental space, when I was in high school. But knowing how I work, which is another thing all those years as the only kid home gave me, I kind of doubt it."

Damn baby sister laying all this truth on me. My throat felt like I'd been kayaking in sea water for a couple of hours, dry and hollow. "I'm glad you found that out. Oh, and you should mention your career goals to Uncle Bill. You need to head him off before he schemes to drop a whole hotel on your life."

"See, and this is how you know I love you. I could save

myself the Uncle Bill hand-me-down problem by encouraging you to settle in with this guy you like and in a job you're okay at. But I don't want that for you. I mean, I do, but only if Cole's made you a pro-con list and you've come to the decision to stay."

Cole's pro-con lists were color coded things of beauty. I'd made him send me the one about taking the Philly job, even though his move was already happening, cause I loved seeing how he'd balanced his way there. It always taught me new ways to approach my own decisions. Plus, it gave us all ideas for his Christmas gifts; if he thought we wouldn't coordinate on a sleek winter wardrobe for him, he didn't truly know his sisters.

"So, you're saying Bill's hotel is not my physics certificate?" Emmeline's bright grin cheered me immensely.

"You knew that already. I'm saying you deserve to eat Greek food whenever you want, and to figure out if following a band across the country or sailing up the Eastern seaboard or dating every choir director in the state of Texas, or somehow all of that, is what makes you feel the most Margo. Because the Margo I see when I look at you is already pretty great, and I want a life for you that allows that greatness to ... to expand so much it'll explode all over us."

Who knew physics majors expressed themselves in such un-scientific ways? But strange visual or not, Emmeline was telling me what I needed to hear. All I had to do was hold on to her words for one more performance, and then I could get on with the plan of not seeing Karl again.

TWENTY-TWO

KARL

Love. It was the theme of the fourth Advent service. As I sat in St. Luke's choir loft, looking down at the congregation, the words of the sermon all resonated in private, personal ways. Ways that were all to do with my own love. With Margo.

Our reverend pointed out how the nativity tableau was focused on Mary and the Wise Men and the Baby Jesus, with Joseph off to the side. And how, without his quiet act of faith that his love for his God put him on the right path, even though it was unexpected and extraordinary, the whole Advent story would change. He'd had the power to destroy Mary's young life, which spoke to a societal misogyny that wasn't as changed now as it should be, but he'd set that aside and worked with his new reality.

I wasn't Joseph. But I was a man who'd thought my life was heading in one direction, and along came love. Would I let it upend everything I'd worked for?

Margo wasn't all I'd been contemplating. I'd also thought about how I'd organized my life around my goals. About missing out on joy by being so focused on my own desires. About if I'd barricaded myself from the rest of the world with my music.

About how Margo had pulled away from me.

About how I'd watched her go.

And now she stood, to all appearances peacefully, with the handbell choir. I was at the piano, accompanying the hymn. I couldn't concentrate, and hoped the uplifted voices of the congregation hid my flubbed notes. Nothing passed over her beautiful face to indicate she'd caught my mistake.

She was young and radiant and full of life, and when she took up her handbells, her focus on the music was absolute. As if nothing urgent and devastating tugged in her, screaming about this being the last song I would ever conduct for her.

As if, as far as she was concerned, I could just retreat after today. Take my music up into my tower of solitude, while she set off to live her life to the fullest.

We closed the service with *Carol of the Bells*. It should have pealed out bright with the love of Christmas, the excitement of Christ's birth, the joyful promise of a better world to come. I didn't know if it rang as hollow to Margo as it did to me, because she continued to avoid my gaze. And instead of following everyone else to the rehearsal room after services, she stopped just inside the parish house to pass her robe and gloves to Matt the Grace, and slipped away before I reached the threshold.

She hadn't answered my texts by the time I met with the Church Council on Monday. Not that I'd expected a reply. Not after her silence each time I reached out, striving to be open without smothering her. Nothing had ever made me feel so old; I'd almost given in and called Aiden for advice, but his serial dating skills weren't what I needed.

"Karl, thanks for accommodating this change of our meeting schedule."

I smiled at the reverend, hoping it was genuine and attentive. "I was a little surprised you wanted to squeeze it in, with everything happening this week."

She smiled back, so that was good. "When am I not busy, though?"

"Good point."

"Besides, this shouldn't take long. Or your part of the meeting shouldn't, I should say."

"I want those parking lot lights," Grace said.

"So do I. It's why we're here. But I also want to balance our budget."

Before their conversation devolved into old territory neither would shift from, I interrupted. "Did you approve my non-budgeted folders?"

It wasn't like me to get straight to the point like that. Margo's influence, maybe. Or my impatience to get back to mournful, meandering drives in my pickup truck with my trusty dog at my side, whichever.

"Yes, we did. The council has voted, and I'm happy to say that your folders are already on order."

I bowed my head in thanks, feeling funny sense of loss settle in my chest, even though I'd been given what I wanted. "I appreciate it."

"Now, the parking lot issue ..."

I tuned out the rest of their conversation, letting my mind drift, inevitably, back to Margo. I wished her all the best, even as I mourned what could have been. She'd been my brightest spot in a long time. My ray of hope that maybe I could find the happiness I craved. But if she wouldn't let me in, if she kept her distance, what did that say about my chances?

I left after promising I'd review the paperwork about the new fiscal year when it hit my inbox. I was tempted to set off on another aimless drive, but that was just delaying reality. I had a job to do, even if it didn't bring me the joy it once did. Until I found it again, I would have to settle for being content.

When I got home, the first thing I saw was the Christmas present I'd found for Margo at the Market Days event we'd once planned to visit together.

It wasn't much; a token, really. I could return it. Or find someone else to give it to. Or stick it in the back of a drawer, and hope that the next time I ran across it, it carried the good memories of being with her. The knowledge that our brief relationship had shifted my perspective, led me to think more deeply about my faith, taught me new songs.

I hadn't given up on us.

The odds were against a way forward for us, at least in the immediate future. And I didn't know if I could chart a new course that wouldn't detract from what we both needed. Either way, I knew one thing for sure.

Margo had changed my life, and I would never forget her.

TWENTY-THREE

MARGO

Everyone was in town for the Dunway holiday party. My sisters, the husbands, Larissa's kids. Cole managed to arrive after the tamalada, the brat, but since Emmeline and I had been jumping in to prep the salsas, pick up the masa and pork and other ingredients, and generally tidy the house, we managed everything without his help.

I still sent some threatening texts about if he thought moving to Philly meant he could get out of hours of spreading dough and fillings on corn husks and folding them so they were ready for the steamer, he was very much mistaken.

Cole finally showed, looking bit sheepish but bearing a six-pack of beer. Emmeline snagged one and took off for her room. He made to follow suit, but I fixed him with a look and said, "Oh, no, you don't. You missed Mama and Aunt Max trying to one-up each other with their chicken fillings. You're on clean-up."

"Ohh, which are Maxima's? I gotta grab one before anyone sees."

"You are going to be in so much trouble." I grabbed my own beer and stuck the rest in the fridge.

"Only if anyone tells on me. Which my favorite sister would never do."

Sarita walked up behind him just then, and I nearly snorted beer through my nose. Cole spun and wrapped her in a hug. "You won't tell on me, right, favorite sister?"

She bopped the back of his head. "You're so lucky Mama is still outside telling Bill and Sam they're messing up the porch lights."

"Ignatius helping them?" I guessed. Ignatius Madigan —or Scorch, as the industry called him—was the slightly more famous of my two rock star brothers-in-law. He and Sarita had fallen for each other a few Christmases back, when he was escaping some wicked publicity by holing up in the elders' rental cottage on the beach. Through the vagaries of family alchemy, he and Uncle Bill had become buds.

Sarita confirmed my guess, then pointed out the tamales he wanted to Cole. Once we all had plates, and our brother promised he'd tackle all the dishes, we retreated to the living room.

"So what happened with Cutie McChoirface?" Cole asked. "And also, please tell me it's over because if three of my sisters run off with musicians, I have to wonder what fate has in store for me and Emmeline."

"I'm a musician, too," Sarita reminded him, though she'd left her school orchestra position after making things permanent with Ignatius.

He waved a hand.

"And Alfie can't even carry a lullaby if you pour it into a nice empty bucket for him," I added.

Cole brushed off the reminder about Larissa's husband, too.

I sighed. "Well, you can stop worrying. Karl and I are over."

Of course, that wasn't a complete enough answer for them. I'd kept all of the details to myself during the tamalada, but now that the elders were congregating on the patio with their own drinks, I told my siblings more. Jeannie wandered in half-way through, along with her husband Brendan, who took a look at our circle of Dunway siblings and slipped out to join Ignatius. I knew both husbands would hear a version of my news later, but it was easier to share without them in the room. I loved them, because they loved my sisters, and also they were great people. But I wasn't up for talking about the sad parts of my dating life with them in the audience.

"And now I'm single again. I mean, the whole thing was less than a month of my life, so it's not even a big story. I don't know why y'all are giving me the inquisition about it. Like I told Emmeline, this frees me up to follow my bliss or whatever. And now Cole and I got the lease situation sorted, there's nothing holding me back."

"Except a destination for this whole adventure of yours. Or even a first step," Cole muttered.

Sarita smacked him on the arm. "Be nice."

"I am being nice," he protested. "I'm just pointing out that Gogo swore she was going to spend this month coming up with a list of possible passions to pursue. She only did the handbells cause I tricked her into it, and she hasn't told me the littlest hint of what comes next. Instead she spent all that thinking time getting hot and heavy with Karl."

"It wasn't just the sex."

"Trust me, we know." Sarita knocked her shoulder into

mine. "You spammed the group text with a thousand pics of his dog."

"Not an euphemism," Cole said.

"Parsley's a good dog." I drained my beer, like it would help me swallow down the pang of missing her comforting weight at my side. "Besides, I've only been at the hotel and church and here otherwise. Parsley was the most interesting thing I could send y'all pictures of."

"We don't need photos to find you worth our time," Cole said with that big-brother-seeing-into-my-soul thing he could do too easily.

"I know that," I said. "But it's not like I had anything else going on in my life."

"You have us," Sarita said gently.

"I know, but." I looked at them all, a bunch of fun-mirror reflections of my face watching me with kindness and love. "I adore all of you, and I love spending time with you. But too often I've let myself exist in your shadows. Four older siblings—it's a lot of shadow, y'all. And you've got your relationships, or your careers, or your communities, or your hobbies. Whatever they are, you've got your things that you're passionate about. And here I am, just kind of muddling through. I can't define myself forever in opposition to or alignment with my big brother and sisters. I need to exist in the sun, away from Rockport, so I can make that list Cole wants from me."

Ignatius cleared his throat as he settled onto the piano bench. I hadn't seen him reenter, though Sarita's smile said she'd been all too aware of his every move. "So. Sorry to interrupt. I was chatting with Emmeline, and we had an idea. But, listen, if it messes with your sunshine thing, there's no pressure, right?"

My pulse quickened as I looked at him. "What is it?"

"You know I'm going on tour soon? It'll be eight months, mostly US dates. I think you should come on with me. Be my assistant."

I was floored. "Ignatius, you're serious?"

"You're organized and decisive, and you're good with people. You know when to be pushy. And I can trust you. I think you'd be perfect. But you'd be stuck spending a lot of time with Sarita, if that's a deal-breaker."

His grin cracked the rest of us up, even while his wife stuck out her tongue. She took my hand, though, squeezing it like she needed me to know she supported this plan.

I hopped up to give him a hug. "When do you start?" My tone didn't reveal any of the ways I was quashing my urge to run to Karl with the news.

We compared calendars and he sent my email to his manager. I'd have a contract to consider by New Year's Eve.

"Travel, work, a little bit of spare time—right, Ignatius? —to think about the things that matter to you. A free trip to Philly to check up on me," Cole said. "It's everything you were looking for, Gogo."

He was looking at me too keenly, and I grabbed all the empty bottles to take to recycling. And then I got started unloading the dishwasher, cause I was absolutely not going to give in to the prick of tears stabbing at my eyes. Not when all the things I'd claimed to want just landed in my lap.

Nothing was stopping me from following this dream. And like I always said, it was the journey that mattered to me. I didn't need destinations: I needed the open road of possibility before me. And now I had it.

It was perfect. I told myself that seven times in a row, hoping it'd stick: this opportunity was perfect.

In the other room, Ignatius started to play. As always,

his music filled the room. I drifted in, ready to let it chase away any residual nonsense aches in my heart. We all sang along, our voices lifting in harmony with his piano, even Jeannie's. For a moment, everything felt right in the world. But eventually the song came to an end, and the couples drifted off together, and Cole took over the kitchen, and where there had been a circle of warmth, now it was just me, quiet, and alone.

TWENTY-FOUR

KARL

I made the mistake of accepting Matt the Grace's invitation to Christmas dinner. It was because of that niece of his, who'd reported to the grapevine about my family traveling over the holiday. And the whole hand-bell choir already knew Margo wasn't including me in her family celebrations.

They knew, because she'd invited all of them to her parents' big party.

So I showed up at Matt the Grace's house on Christmas, utterly out of place among the crowd. Tempted to find a quiet corner, as if I was visiting my own family. The problem with that plan was the lack of quiet corners. His house was all glittering lights and garlands on the door-ways and festive touches and strangers whose names I'd missed while trying to find where to place my bowl of fruit salad.

In the midst of it all, Matt the Grace and his wife look perfectly at ease. She rounded up a few people so I could explain why we all called her husband Matt the Grace.

"That's not his legal name?" I deadpanned.

Paul jumped in. "Until I started ringing with them, I was sure he was exaggerating about the name. But every one of them calls him Matt the Grace, like they've never heard any different."

"Well, most of them haven't." I sipped my eggnog. "But first of all, we do have two people named Grace in the handbell choir. The three of them were the only ones who showed up for my first ringers' rehearsal. Before long, Matt said I should just call all of them Grace to stop me stumbling over who I was trying to talk to."

"You didn't call us anything," Matt the Grace jumped in, because the man didn't miss a chance to be contradictory. "I had to do something or my permanent church name would have been D5 E5."

I laughed with the crowd, who seemed to understand at least the basics of music notation. "Nah, once we had a few other ringers, I'd have started calling you B4 C5."

Matt the Grace flexed to show off his low bell ringer's arm muscles, and took the center of attention away from me. Thank goodness.

His son Paul guided me to the appetizers and I shook off my mood. "Thanks."

"You looked a little in need of rescue."

"That obvious?"

He winced a little. "There's a Three Graces text thread that Dad insisted on reading aloud after Margo's party. I made all of them promise: no trying to set you up until spring at least."

I palmed my face. "Fantastic."

He shifted a bit. "Sorry. It's so weird, because outside of choir, Dad isn't the type to meddle, but when he and the other Graces get together ..."

"Yeah, I know. You're fine. They're fine." I stopped short of claiming I was fine, since we both knew it would be a lie.

Margo wasn't in a place to want the things I did. She had places to go with her life, and mine was right here, rooted in Rockport. I didn't need to explain all that to Paul. He obviously knew enough to make him sympathetic. Or maybe my eyes radiated the kind of sadness people thought it politer to not mention.

Paul hustled off to check on his side dishes, and I found a spot tucked beside the Christmas tree to linger, studying what was clearly decades of homemade ornaments. I'd always presumed that someday, I'd have a similar collection to replace generic baubles on the short artificial tree I'd anchored in the living room in case Parsley's tail knocked it over.

Right now the only personalized ornaments hanging on it were a framed picture of Parsley's first Christmas, and the bell I'd gotten Margo and never had a chance to gift her. It was all another opportunity to question the assumptions I'd build up about my life.

I managed to slip away before dinner was served. Matt the Grace walked me out, promising to return my fruit salad bowl in the new year.

"I'm sorry if my family was more than you bargained for," he said as we approached my truck. "I love them, but they can be a little overwhelming."

I mustered a smile. "They're great."

And that was the truth. I was used to being the outsider, the one who didn't quite fit in. It didn't bother me as much as it used to. I had my friends, and my dog, and that was enough. I didn't need an invite to my sister's team road trip, or a particular woman with streaks of bright color in her dark hair, to celebrate a holiday with me. I was full up on eggnog and cheese balls and gingerbread, and Matt the Grace insisted I take a foil-covered plate home with me.

"There's always room for one more at our table," he said. "It doesn't have to be a holiday."

I should have been touched, but all I could think was that if this established family could always be so flexible and welcoming, maybe making perfect fits was the wrong goal. If I wanted Margo—and I did want Margo—I had to tumble down that tower she said I'd built, and walk back to her on my own two feet.

I didn't have to be a Grace, and I didn't have to settle for someone who wasn't Margo. We could find our own way together, even if that meant leaving this town I'd hoped would become my own. But what felt important for my future wasn't my job, and wasn't Rockport, and wasn't staying a carefully proscribed distance from my parents.

I'd mixed all that up with my longing for heart-string things like my dog, my music, and my future collection of handmade ornaments. And most importantly, for the partner who would share it all. Who would help me truly find out what it felt like to belong.

So Merry Christmas to me, and to the faith that lifted me up while I worked out a new way to go after my dreams.

CHAPTER

TWENTY-FIVE

MARGO

Sky, waves, the mist of the sea. A grey horizon stretched wide in front of me. I'd started my day early, packing a dry bag and picking up the single-person sea kayak from Mama and Dad's garage.

In a couple of days, I'd drive up to Austin to sort out the apartment, and help Cole with the last couple of things before his flight. Then I'd return to Rockport for my last couple of weeks working for Uncle Bill.

And then? Then I was on my own.

To mark this long-awaited transition, I was kayaking out into the Gulf of Mexico to watch the sun rise on the last day of the year. There was a mild chop, so paddling took some concentration, muscles stretching and pulling across my back. The morning dawned cold and overcast; sunlight crept slowly across the low clouds. Finally, I rested the oar across my lap and uncapped my thermos of green tea, watching for hints of orange or pink to peek through the sky. The colors were slow to emerge, but as I sipped the slightly bitter brew, I began to make out more waves in the distance. The salt-brine scent of the Gulf was getting

133

stronger, or my senses were waking up. I was close enough to still find the lights of Rockport and Fulton behind me, but not far enough to make out any of St. Jo ahead of me.

A very in the middle place to be.

But not a bad place. I sat there for a while, sipping my tea and watching the world come alive around me. The sun rose higher in the sky, eventually burning through the clouds and painting the waves with gold. Schools of fish darted just below the surface. A pelican soared by, low over the water.

Time seemed to slow down as I sat there, lost in thought. What would the next year bring? I was finally able to imagine some shape to my journey. And I knew what I would be missing, which was another kind of shape entirely.

I pushed away the melancholy, just like I'd pushed away every urge to text Karl back. To keep discussing round and round the same problems.

Eventually, I paddled back to shore and pulled my kayak up onto the beach. Shaking out my arms, I looked back from where I'd come. The day was still cloudy, but the grays had given way to purples and whites and oranges.

While hefting the boat to carry it to the car, I barely had time to brace before a tumult of golden fur raced across the sand and barreled into me.

"Parsley," Karl called from the parking lot. She wasn't paying him much mind, except for how she was guiding me towards him. And he was approaching me in return.

"Karl." I sounded cautious, which irritated me. I didn't like having reason for caution.

"Sorry, hi. I wasn't trying to ambush you. Do you want help with the kayak?"

I shook my head. I'd grabbed the closest parking spot to

the launch pad, thanks to no one else getting up so early on a cold-dark December morning. Parsley kept pace with me as I got the kayak onto my roof rack, so I was extra-careful to keep us both safe from falls.

Instead of tying down the boat, I turned and crossed my aching arms across my chest. "What is this, if not an ambush?"

All those wisps of golden sun found their way to his face and hair. He gleamed like a living statue, and I resisted another urge, curling my fists so I wouldn't touch him.

"We were driving out to the airport park. I promised her a run on the dunes. But then I saw your car, and ... just stopped. It was like I crashed landed in the parking lot, and I needed to be still and get my bearings for a sec. You weren't in your car, so we've been walking the beach. Waiting. Hoping."

I crouched to pat Parsley. "It sounds a little like an ambush."

From down at sand level, I watched him shift back to lean against the hood of my car. "Yeah, I get that. It is an ambush. It just wasn't my plan to track you down. Not yet. Not like this. If I'd planned—"

I gazed up his body, clad in jeans and a flannel shirt I knew to be nearly as soft as Parsley's ears. Slowly, I rose and faced him, setting a hand on that comforting warm curve of the dog's head. "Not yet?"

He sighed, scrubbing a hand through his hair. "Yeah. I wanted to do this right. You know? But it's been weeks, and I've missed you, and there was your car, like a beacon I couldn't ignore. Plus, Parsley really wanted to say hi."

"Parsley did?" The question came out more tenderly than I'd intended, but I couldn't take it back now.

She wagged at me as if to prove Karl wasn't using her to

deflect whatever this was. I scratched her ears, directing my reluctant smile entirely at her.

"No, not just Parsley. I miss you. I said that, but you can't imagine how true it is. I miss your touch, and your determination, and the joy of sitting with you over a meal. I miss singing with you. How you curse freely. The color in your hair. I miss your strength, Margo. Your kindness."

Good thing I'd lifted the kayak to the roof already. My whole torso felt wobbly. Under my rash guard I was all goosebumps. I didn't know what to say, so I didn't even try.

Karl, though, had all the words. "It's not that my house is too empty now. It's not that you're a generic beautiful woman and I could just go out and find a—a convenient replacement. There's no convenient replacement for you, because you're not convenient, Margo. You are so inconvenient."

I had to laugh. "Karl."

"That sounds wrong, but it's also so true. You're perfectly inconvenient, and the past couple of weeks without you have only shown me exactly what a Margo-shaped piece is missing from my life. You don't need to fit into my pattern, because, and I didn't even realize I was doing it, I threw out that puzzle. It wasn't right for my life. It didn't make room for you as you are, but more than that —it's not who I am anymore. You talk about destinations as bad because they're static, and what I figured out I did was make my destination so fixed in place I couldn't see how I'd trapped myself in it."

"Karl." I wasn't laughing now. I closed the distance between us. "This is the sweetest ambush, but it doesn't fix everything. I got this job—"

"I heard. Congratulations." He tried threading his fingers through my ocean-thick hair and failed, but his still managed to slip his palm around to cradle my neck. The familiar heat of his body near mine grounded me.

"How'd you know?"

On a huff of air, he tilted his forehead to mine. "Quiet Grace texted me. She really likes to remind us that not speaking much doesn't mean she's not opinionated."

I got my hands on that soft shirt. Traced the hard muscles of his upper arms. "She really is."

"She's the one who told me about your job, too. It's great, Margo. Are you excited?"

My heart was lurching towards his. I swallowed. "It's all the things I said I wanted."

Trust Karl, who could hear one flat note in a chorus, to catch the hitch in my words. His own voice was low and rough when he asked, "That you said you wanted, or that you do want?"

I waited before answering. Not because I didn't know the answer, but because we weren't really talking about who worked where. Those logistics only mattered if we'd addressed everything underneath them.

"I'm not taking the job, not until I know if there's a way forward for us, too. I've been round and over it, and I don't know how it would look, but maybe we can figure it out together? And I don't mean eight months of long distance or constantly flying between the tour and Rockport, if that's the thought that made your eyes light up. We need better plans, and I still don't want to settle for this town."

He nodded. "I understand. And ... yes, on figuring it out together. I want that chance with you. The chance to be your partner."

I rushed out more concerns. "And it'll be years before I'm ready to have kids. If I got pregnant today, I'd termi-nate. I'm not going to want to recreate the big families we come from. All credit to my parents, but six children is ridiculous."

Karl's smile broke across his face as bright as sunlight on the waves. "Agreed. But Margo, you might find your life is full enough without children. Or maybe we'll find we can't have kids, can't for whatever reason expand our family past the two of us."

"The two of us, and my brother and sisters, and your siblings, and our cousins, and my godparents, and our parents, and my brothers-in-law and their managers, and your sister's teammates, and the Graces, I'm sure."

"And Parsley."

At her name, the dog wedged her nose between our legs. I wiped dry my cheeks. "And Parsley."

Karl closed his eyes, then opened them and let me see every feeling shining from their depths. "Margo, I love you."

I didn't need to wait before answering him. I kissed him once, fierce and firm. "I love you, too."

CHAPTER

TWENTY-SIX

KARL

Epiphany Sunday was my last as an employee of St. Luke's. Everyone was generous with their praise, both from the pulpit and afterwards, in the courtyard, with a chocolate sheet cake to accompany our usual tea and coffee social time.

After one last check that I'd left everything tidy for my successor, I locked up my office in the parish house and handed over the key to Church Council Grace. Matt the Grace wrapped me in a long hug, and Quiet Grace kissed both Margo and I.

"You want to go to Semaphore?" I asked as we collected Parsley and set off.

Margo shook her head. "How about instead we just go home?"

On New Year's Day, we'd driven up to Austin to clear the rest of her stuff out of her apartment. She'd sold the furniture Cole didn't want to the new tenant, and everything else fit in the back of my truck. Once we'd dropped Cole at the airport, we returned to Rockport and transferred her remaining possessions from the hotel and her parents' house, to mine.

Ours.

Cole teased us about jumping into living together so fast, but since Ignatius's tour started right after Valentine's Day, we weren't going to live in my house much at all. He'd offered tour bus space for me and Parsley, but I'd be back and forth depending on my gig work. I'd reached out to churches in all his tour cities, and already lined up several coinciding dates where I would be stepping in as a sub for vacationing choir directors. On top of that, I was playing in a few festivals, offering a series of handbell clinics, and had adapted my home mixing studio set-up to be road ready. It was enough to pay my mortgage and keep Parsley in kibble as Margo and I figured out how to balance traveling and working together.

I wasn't worried about it. I hadn't second-guessed a moment since New Year's Eve, when I'd paced the beach watching her kayak approach, fearing she'd cast my love out with the tide. Fearing that I was leaping from a discontented safety, not into a terrifyingly new rightness, but into a prickly desolation.

But I'd landed in bliss.

She loved me back.

"What's that smile for?" Margo asked.

I flashed her a significant look and waggled my eyebrows. She broke into a grin and started to jog the rest of the way home. Parsley bounded after her, and I followed more slowly, enjoying the sight of Margo's dark hair and Parsley's bright fur streaming behind them as they approached our home.

I'd unbuttoned my cuffs and pulled off my tie by the time I locked the door, shutting us in. Margo waited for me in the threshold of the office, boots kicked off and long skirt already skimming down her curves.

"Were you planning to seduce me?" I teased.

"No," she said, sauntering closer and sliding her arms around my neck. "I was just going to let you take me."

I couldn't resist a delighted laugh as I swept her into my arms and kissed her deeply. She tasted like tea and sunshine, and I lost myself in the sweetness of her mouth as my hands roamed over her body.

We moved to the futon, shedding clothes along the way. Margo lay back, watching me with half-lidded eyes as I gazed down at her. Her skin was soft and luscious, her hair a dark halo around her head. She looked like a goddess, her body made for me to worship.

We came together slowly, our kisses lazy, luxurious. We had all day. We had weeks, and months. We had years. I kissed her with the weight of our future between us, and she held me to her like it was forever.

Each gentle undulation of her hips into mine built the urgency between us. We had all the time, yes, but I needed her pleasure now. I slid out of her hold and spread her legs.

"Karl," she gasped as I lowered my head.

I didn't answer, lost in the perfection of her body. In the slick heat of her desire on my tongue. I teased her clit, tasting and thumbing and thrumming until she shook on the edge of orgasm. Then I backed off, relishing her frustrated protest as evidence that she trusted me with her desire. I needed that desire; it gave my soul wings.

I nipped each trembling thigh, and went back to the center of my joy. Her sheath pulled against my thrusting fingers, and my cock throbbed in anticipation. But that bliss could wait; Margo's orgasm couldn't. I licked and sucked until she was coming hard on my tongue, arching into me, her hands tangling in my hair as we found her release.

I nuzzled my way up her body and claimed the kiss she offered me.

"That was," she breathed, "amazing."

I grinned and kissed her again. "I aim to please."

"Speaking of please, would you please fuck me right this instant?"

I didn't need to be asked twice. I aligned our bodies and pushed forward until we were both gasping for air. Margo's tight heat surrounded me, and I fought to keep the pounding urgency at bay as we rocked together. The bliss was exquisite, but it wouldn't last long at this rate.

So I took her hard and fast, giving in to the need that drove us both. Margo's hands clenched on my back as she cried out in ecstasy, her body bowing beneath me as she found her pleasure again. I followed suit with a hiss of satisfaction, pumping deep into her as my climax tore through me.

We collapsed together, trembling and sweaty and weak with the force of what we'd shared. Neither of us spoke as our heartbeats slowed and our breathing returned to normal. Margo traced patterns on my chest with one finger, and I stroked my hand up and down her spine.

This was peace, and faith.

This was love, and joy.

This was home.

EPILOGUE
MARGO

"Parsley!" I crouched so our dog could hurtle into my arms. I'd missed her. Karl had been back and forth over the first couple of months of the tour, but we'd found it was too much traveling for Parsley, who'd come to love hanging out with Aiden whenever Karl was out of town.

"Stop hogging my puppers and go kiss your guy," Ignatius said, grabbing Parsley's leash like I wasn't the one who'd brought the beloved dog into his life.

"I thought you wanted to review the set up of the voter registration and fair housing tables for this week's venues?"

Ignatius blew out an unconcerned breath. "You probably did it right. Anyone who this perfect dog kisses and who thought up the action booths to start with probably gets the details right."

I laughed and took the win, and my brother-in-law took the dog towards his bandmates. I wrapped myself into Karl's arms. "How was the drive?"

The New Orleans late spring heat shone down on us,

but it was his kiss that raised my temperature. "Too long. Fine. But too long. Where's our room?"

I laughed. "Glad to see your stamina wasn't drained by the hours crossing the swamplands."

"Stopped for coffee at the border, bought Parsley a squeaky alligator at a gas station, all very adventurous. Now I need to collapse my road-weary bones onto a bed so you can have your wicked way with me."

I pulled him towards the entrance of the guesthouse, our steps echoing on the cobblestones as we hurried to get inside. I'd barely had time to check in before Karl arrived, and now all I wanted was to get him upstairs so I could finally touch him again. My skin prickled with anticipation under his hand at my back.

Once in the room, we tumbled onto the four-poster bed, Karl pulling me on top of him. His hands roamed my body, exploring every inch of me as if we'd been apart for months, not weeks. I understood the feeling; getting to his skin was my highest priority. "Love you," I said between desperate kisses.

"Love you, Margo. Take off this dress."

I whipped it over my head and let it sail across the room. He settled himself between my legs, and I moaned as he entered me. We moved together, faster and faster, tumbling and racing towards climax.

After, collapsed together and watching the ceiling fan rotate above us, Karl cleared his throat. "I have a plan."

I reached for his hand. "Yeah?"

He squeezed. "Only if it doesn't get in your way." He was always careful about encroaching. Letting me know what he wanted, but also that he could step back if necessary. Increasingly, I was sure it was something I would never need.

"Let's hear it."

"I've lined up gigs in the Twin Cities and St. Louis, and workshops in Philly and Nashville. It's enough, with everything else, that I can stay with you until the tour's over. I packed everything we'd need, just in case. And Aiden said if I fly him up here and get him a ticket to Scorch's show, he'll drive my truck back home."

I tugged him to me. "Really?"

He stroked my hair behind my ear, eyes soft. "Margo, of course, really."

"I worried you were tired of tour bus life."

"Spending all my time with you, and about two dozen people around to help us spoil Parsley when we want to sneak off together? What would I be tired of?"

I looked around the eclectic, charming bedroom, all antiques and regional art. "Not being in your own home? Missing time with your friends? Cobbling together jobs to support all this?"

"Are you tired of any of that?" He sounded only curious, not like he hoped for any particular answer.

I took a deep breath. Blew it out slowly while I shook my head. "I love it. This tour's been everything I hoped for. But only because I got to share it with you."

He cradled me down beside him, floating the sheet up and letting it settle over our entwined bodies. "I love it, too. When we started, I only hoped for time for us to learn all the contours of our relationship. But it's been so much more. I've stretched into new ways of making a living, and discovered places I never thought to visit, and, mostly, I've had time to admire all that you are. You make everything fascinating, Margo. You jump in with both feet, no matter what it is. I want to keep jumping in with you, for as long as we can."

I grinned and leaned in for a kiss. "Then it's a plan."

* * *

THANKS FOR RINGING *your way to love with* Margo of the Bells. *Reviews are an invaluable tool for authors, and I'd love to get your honest review at any of the following places, or others of your choosing:*

*Stores * Goodreads * Bookbub*

FOR A COMPLETE BOOK *list and more, keep scrolling. You can also check out Sarita & Scorch's meet-ouch in the enclosed sample chapter.*
Happy reading!
-Melanie

Acknowledgments

The Dunway Siblings are back! I have such fun with this family, and with the gender-flipped fairy tales that inspire their love stories. (Okay, I admit Rapunzel wasn't the strongest mapping option, but poor Karl was trapped in a tower and needed me to find a way to rescue him.)

I couldn't have brought Margo to the page without the constant support of my family. Robert, as always, is the best. I also appreciate my dad for having an 80th birthday that worked as a convenient deadline during a sometimes tough and always scattered year. Thanks for always holding up "love you more" as a real-life standard for romance.

This story benefited from the brilliant editorial advice of Jennifer Prokop; Jen, thanks for the guidance, insight, and encouragement. I'm also grateful for the kindness and expertise of my sensitivity editor David Pena, and for Karen's sweet, prompt proofreading.

About the Author

Melanie Greene lives in a tiny woodland cottage in a big skyscraper city, with her husband and kids and pets and plants and all the people inhabiting her imagination.

For more info, visit her at www.melaniegreene.com, where you can sign up for her newsletter to access new releases and bonus content.

 facebook.com/MelGreeneBooks

 twitter.com/Daki_MelGreene

 instagram.com/melaniegreeneauthor